Lissie Pendle

By Ian Burns

Scratcher (First *Niamong* book)
   Illustrated by Bruce Rankin

Lissie Pendle (Second *Niamong* book)

Possum and Python

The Alone Man

The Search for Quong (Third *Niamong* book)

Thomas Bulford's English Companion

Thomas Bulford's Essays on Life, Language & Love

Ranga Plays Australia (Fourth *Niamong* book)

The Day and Night Machine

Twevven and the horrible big bigger biggest
baby burp
   Illustrated by Lauren Eldridge-Murray

Twevven in a very dangerous situation
   Illustrated by Lauren Eldridge-Murray

The Package on the Tram (Sequel to *The Day
and Night Machine*)

The Wisdom of Harkishen Singh

Lissie Pendle

or

Some Funny Things Happen to a Country Kid on the Way
to Growing Up

Ian B G Burns

Published by Imaginal Works 2009

Copyright Ian B G Burns 2005

National Library of Australia Cataloguing-in-Publication:

Burns, Ian, 1939-

ISBN 9780994597649

Lissie Pendle: some funny things happen to a country kid on the way to growing up/Ian Burns.

Series: Niamong books

Dewey Number: A823.4

Cover design: Jess Gilmore

Cover illustrations: Bruce Rankin

Web: www.twevven.com

Email: ibgburns@gmail.com

For Elissa, whose idea it was

CONTENTS

1

Me

...where I tell you about me.

If there's one thing I don't mind doing, it's agreeing with myself. And if there's one thing I really agree with myself about nearly all the time it's that it's tough *al*ways being a girl.

For boys it's different. For them life is one great pram ride. For them it's like living in an armchair, all soft and warm, with big, comfortable arms to rest on. As long as their mothers keep up the supply of food they couldn't care less about anything. Especially girls.

It's not like that with me. I really like boys, or *some* boys, anyway. Jingo's my favourite boy at school, in fact *he*'s my favourite boy *any*where because all the boys in Niamong go to my school.

Imagine nearly thirty boys all together in one place at the same time! It'd be like going into Mrs Macleod's lolly shop on the main street and being able to choose the best ones from all those big glass jars on the shelves. You go in the door and the bell rings over your head and Mrs Macleod waddles out from the back where she's been socking into cream and raspberry jam sponge (you can tell, because most of it's still hanging from her chin) and you stand there, choosing.

I never choose quickly because that'd mean paying the money too soon and having to leave before I'd let my eyes have a proper feast. I'd walk slowly along the counter, checking out each jar, with Mrs Macleod shuff-ling on the other side to make sure that I didn't snaffle any lollies while she wasn't looking. I never bought the same lollies I'd had the week before and one day I'm going to try to have a different one every week for a year.

School isn't quite as good as the lolly shop, though. In the first place you *have* to go to school, at least until you're old enough to leave. In the second place, which is just about in the same place as the first place, most of the boys are too young for me, and in any case they're not sweet.

What's the good of having nearly thirty boys to choose from if most of them are still wearing nappies? Well, that's not ex*act*ly true, even though I've seen a few boys around with their shorts looking a little damp in front. Especially when Mr Braden's in one of his tempers.

Still, with Jingo being there I'm pretty happy generally, except that it's hard trying to get him to talk to me when anyone else is around. I don't think that Jingo is his real name – that's just what everybody calls him. I think that maybe his real name is one that he doesn't like very much, or maybe he's just forgotten what it is. Whatever it is, I can't forget *him*.

The best time I've had with him was when we were all coming back from rabbiting, on the back of Old Mary, the biggest horse in Australia. We were all tired out and I leaned my head on Jingo's shoulder and went to sleep. The horse lumbered along, and even walked through a dam, and Jingo didn't push my head off or say anything.

It was lucky that he didn't realise that I was just pretending. Pretending to be asleep, that is. Not pretending about the snuggle.

I don't know why boys don't like talking to girls when other people are around. After all, we come from the same place, almost. And all we want to do is give them a cuddle or, perhaps, a little kiss or two. Or three or four in Jingo's case.

Last year we went down to Melbourne for the Christmas holidays and I didn't see Jingo for six whole weeks. I nearly died. I couldn't ring him up, because I didn't know his phone number. And, anyway, I don't think he had a phone. That was one of the troubles with living in Niamong instead of America. We had one, but who could I ring up there? Not Jingo or Jemmy or Scratcher. One or two girls had one, but who'd want to ring *them*?

Why don't boys just come out into the open and say they like us? It would make things so much easier for us and I'm sure that they'd be much happier. After all, girls are quite special. We're intelligent and beautiful, and can say lots of interesting things when we get going, and know how to read and write and do terrific borders around our pages at school, and we can cook and sew and ride bikes and horses, and even tractors, and play rounders and netball – all these are things boys should appreciate.

Instead, whenever you start talking about them they start sniggering. Jingo doesn't really do that, though, except when other boys are around, and even then I think he has his fingers crossed behind his back or in his pocket. Maybe one day when I'm really old and the boys are even older they won't need to snigger, but I doubt it. Boys can be so dumb.

I was glad that for at least some of my life we didn't have a boy in our family, if you didn't count Dad. Having someone around to boss about is all right but young brothers are really not worth the trouble. Still, I suppose having an older brother would be even worse. He'd be strutting around the house making out he was great and better at everything than Dad (which wouldn't be all that hard sometimes, but you know what I mean), and spending all the time in front of the bathroom mirror on Saturday nights brushing his eyebrows and putting Mum's perfume under his arms before the dance down at the Returned Services League hall – the RSL. That'd really make me sick.

If you take my advice, then, don't have any brothers in your family. Unless you're Jingo's sister, of course. I'd love to be Jingo's sister, and then I'd see him every day and night, especially in the holidays. On the other hand, if I was Jingo's sister there's just a chance, even with him, that he might be like all the rest and I'd hate him. No, I don't think I could ever hate Jingo; he's so nice, with his hair tossed over his left eye because of the strong wind. He's so manly, but not like most of the men I know, who don't seem to know how to talk to girls unless they're handing over glasses of beer in the Lalor's Arms. Not that I go in there, but I bet that's what it's like.

Most of the boys in our school aren't too bad, except for the McPhees. The worst thing that can happen at school is for Mr Braden to put you in a group with the McPhees to do a project. They live with pigs and ferrets. Pigs aren't too bad – they just grunt and roll in the mud and put their noses and feet in their dinner. The McPhees do all of those things, but they also smell like their ferrets, and if you've ever smelled a ferret, let alone a dozen, you'll know that there are easier ways of winning a war than dropping bombs. You'd just send out the McPhees, making sure the wind's blowing towards the enemy. It's not that they never have a bath – they haven't *got* a bath, and the copper in their laundry is only used for making stuff their father drinks when he isn't out working in the paddocks, which is most of the time.

Boys have all the fun, too. They're allowed to go off blackberrying in the bush whenever they want to, even when there aren't any blackberries. They just go off for hours on end and no one at home seems to give them a thought. I suppose it's because parents know that their sons'll always be home for tea, even if they've got two broken legs and a squashed nose. 'What've you been up to, son?' they'd say. 'Oh, just blackberrying,' would be the reply as the cripple tucked into roast lamb and potatoes. It makes me sick.

Why don't boys have the same rules as girls?

Whenever I want to do something that all the boys in Niamong do without asking anyone I have to yell and stamp my feet and sometimes roll on the floor in a pink rage until I almost believe it myself...or else I just go off and do it and hope my parents worry themselves sick about me; except that I don't often give them much thought when I don't have to worry about them.

Parents seem to have another set of rules altogether, and I can't quite work out what they are. They're so selfish. 'Rules are made to help us,' says Dad, and then he makes *me* go to bed at 8:30. *He* doesn't go to bed at 8:30, nor does Mum; they both stay up to all hours, talking in the lounge, having cups of tea or port, and sometimes, I bet, a bit of a cuddle.

I don't really think that parents should cuddle each other; it's not right and I get terribly embarrassed if they do it when I'm around. I just have to look somewhere else until they've finished and my cheeks can cool down. Sometimes they do it for so long in the kitchen that the peas get burnt and I have to go outside and play with my lamb or chickens.

There should be a rule that they only do it at night, or when I'm away on holidays somewhere. They're too old for it, anyway, and they should grow up and act responsibly.

Jingo says his parents are the same, and so does Jemmy out at Quimbilong. Scratcher doesn't know anything about what his mum and dad do, except that one of them feeds him and the other one whacks him. He's one of the funniest kids around but he's always getting into some sort of trouble. Quite often he finds it hard to sit down and keep still in class.

Why should you have to sit still in class, anyway?

Mr Braden doesn't. In fact he hardly ever sits down. He's always on the prowl somewhere, looking for trouble, and at *our* school he usually finds it. At least *he* calls it trouble — *we* call it fun and try to get into it as often as we can without getting caught.

About the only time Mr Braden sits down is when he's doing the school bank on Wednesday mornings and he has to make sure he doesn't make a mistake in adding up. I think he's scared stiff of the bank manager coming up to school and telling him in front of the whole class that he can't do his sums.

It almost happened once.

Mr Braden had just finished writing in all the bank books, he'd stacked the coins in little piles on his table, and he'd written the total in the special bank book for the school when Scratcher suddenly yelled, 'I've got a blood doze!!'

Mr Braden and the rest of us looked up and saw World War 2 at the back of the room. Blood was everywhere. On the desk, on Scratcher's books and clothes, even, I think, in the ink well.

'All right! Who's bashed Macneill?'

Macneill was Scratcher's proper name, the one he was called by Mr Braden and Miss Hendley and his parents, and one or two other people in Niamong.

'Who's bashed Macneill up in class, I said!'

No-one said anything, because that would've meant trouble without the fun first.

Mr Braden stalked down to Scratcher, each of us moving in towards the middle of our desks as he went past.

'Who bashed you, Macneill, and why were you counting when I was counting the money?!'

'Dobody ad I wased whed you were,' gulped Scratcher, swallowing something which I'd rather not say here.

'You're lying again, Macneill!! I've had to speak to you before about that! I think you'd better come to my office and meet my little friend!'

Mr Braden didn't have any friends, so you can imagine what he was talking about.

'Excuse me, Mr Braden,' I said.

For some reason the classroom went even quieter than it was before.

'She interrupted Mr Braden!' I heard Jemmy whisper behind me.

'She has no fear,' said Jingo in a low voice.

My face went red with joy.

'Yes, Lissie?' Mr Braden barked.

Jingo'd said I was brave, when all I'd done was to speak to Mr Braden.

'*Miss* Pendle! What do you want?!'

Mr Braden was yelling my name! Why? What did he want? Everyone was looking at me, the only sound in the room a plop or two as the blood dripped out of Scratcher's nose and fell onto a bit of paper.

'It was about Scratcher,' said Jingo in my ear.

Oh yes! That was it. I'd very bravely interrupted Mr Braden because of Scratcher.

'Please, Mr Braden. No-one bashed him. It's just that it's a hot day.' And it was. We all had on our lightest clothes, even though that makes no difference in a Niamong summer.

'Oh,' said Mr Braden, 'are you sure?'

'Yes, Mr Braden. It's happened to him before. I'll take him out to the sick bay if you like.'

Mr Braden looked at all the blood. 'All right,' he said, 'and you'd better clean him up a bit, too.' Being a doctor's daughter isn't always a good idea.

Scratcher and I walked out of the classroom and down the corridor towards the sick bay, Scratcher stopping outside Miss Hendley's room for a rest on the way.

'OK, Scratcher, let's have a look at the blood nose.'

'What blood nose?' he asked.

I noticed that he didn't say doze that time. It must've stopped bleeding. Still, when a blood nose stops bleeding it's usually still clogged up with a great big long red.....you know, and you still have to say 'doze'. Something smelt fishy.

'It's tomato sauce.'

Uh oh, another Scratcher piece of mischief. But what a piece! Jingo'd called me brave, when all I'd done was interrupt Mr Braden! Scratcher'd set up the trick, and on Mr Braden of all people! He was the brave one!

'It's tomato sauce! We're going to trick Braden into making a mistake with his bank!'

'How's that going to happen?! He'll never make a mistake!'

'He won't, but Jingo will!!!'

My funny bone crashed into the doorknob, electrifying my fingers. It was all right having Scratcher getting into trouble again, but not Jingo, too!

'When Braden goes down to clean up all the mess on my desk Jingo's going to race out the front and put another penny on someone's pile! Braden'll never notice, and then the bank manager'll come up and roar the tripe out of him for not adding up the money properly!!'

'What if Jingo gets caught?!'

'He won't – he's too quick. I can't wait to see old Braden's face when the bank manager comes in! Boy, it'll go puce and pink and he might even wet . . . his . . ..'

Scratcher's voice trailed off and I looked at him to see why, and there was Mr Braden in the door, behind me, blood on his hands and cuffs. I knew that it wasn't real blood, and I also knew that it would be real blood pretty soon.

'IT'S JUST THAT IT'S A HOT DAY IS IT?! IT'S HAPPENED TO HIM BEFORE HAS IT?! I SUPPOSE THAT WHEN HE'S GOT A BAD COLD HE BLOWS OUT TOMATO SAUCE, DOES HE?!'

He knew about the tomato sauce!

'AND I FOUND THIS CREATURE SNEAKING OUT TOWARDS MY DESK!!' he shouted as he dragged an ear out from behind him, an ear attached to my poor Jingo!

'She didn't.....ow....know.....ouch....any.....oo.....thing......about..uh...itit, Mr Braden....eek!'

'DON'T LIE TO ME! All of you down to the office!!'

I won't tell you any more about that time because it was too painful. And then we had to go back and clean up the classroom.

That was one of the few when I wished that girls had different rules from boys.

Still, I *did* spend the afternoon with Jingo!

2

Little Brothers

...where the worst thing happens.

I wasn't even four when it happened. I'd heard plenty of times Dad saying he was going off to deliver a baby, but this time he BROUGHT ONE HOME.

What was the big idea? Why hadn't they told me? It was my house, too. Who needed someone else in the house anyway? I didn't. I was pretty comfortable, with a nice bedroom and a spare room for when Mum finally allowed one of my friends to come to stay with me, whenever that was going to be. Every time I asked her she said that I was too young or the friend was too young or she and Dad were going over to see Aunt Muriel at Colbinabbin and she wasn't too young but I didn't really want her to stay the night even if she did.

I'd been watching Mum for some time. At first I thought that I was wrong, then I thought that I mightn't be wrong, and then I knew I was right. Mum was getting fat.

As soon as I realised what was happening I started to keep an eye on Dad. But nothing seemed to be happening to him: he stayed as skinny as ever. Sometimes he used to slip out the flywire door without even opening it, and everyone in Niamong used to call him in to rescue kittens stuck under their houses.

All his patients, well, the grown-up ones, called him 'Pencil Pendle', and sometimes even 'Blacklead' (but not usually when he was there).

Dad stayed skinny but Mum didn't. She fatted. She rested her tummy on the table. She started to walk like an elephant; she even ate millions of peanuts, but not with her nose. Dad didn't seem at all worried, but he probably hadn't noticed, or was too embarrassed to say anything to her. *I* would have to do something. It wasn't fair that Dad should marry Mum when she was young and pretty and then have her turn into a wombat.

When Mum was serving up the Sunday roast after church one day I slipped a potato off her plate when she wasn't looking, and gave it to Brissy, but it didn't make any difference.   The next week she was just as bad, even badder.

I tried taking two potatoes off, then three, but she caught me and whacked my bottom for being greedy. And she got fatter. Although it was funny, really, because she was only getting fat around the middle, not her face or arms.

And then one morning I came in to breakfast and found nothing there except Dad, and he looked as though he'd been up all night.

'Where's Mummy?' I said. (I hadn't started to call her Mum yet.)

'She's in the base hospital.'

Hospital! I knew there was something wrong with her!

'She's died of fat, hasn't she?!'

'No, she hasn't.'

'It was all those potatoes, wasn't it! I tried to stop her eating so many. And all those peanuts!'

'She wasn't fat.'

'She was as fat as a house! I wanted to tell you she was getting fat, but I couldn't!'

'I knew what was happening.'

'You didn't want to tell her because you were too embarrassed, or you didn't want to hurt her feelings!'

'Everybody gets like that when they're having a baby."

'A baby! Why was she getting fat because she was having a baby?! What's having a baby got to do with getting fat?!!"

'The baby was growing in her tummy.'

'In her tummy!!! With all those peanuts!!!?'

'Well, next to her tummy.'

'Next to her tummy?! How'd it get in there? Did she eat it, too? Is that why she was so fat? Where'd she get the baby from and how did it get down into next to her tummy?? How did it breathe in there?! Why didn't I hear it crying? How did you change its nappies?? How did you give it its bottle?!? Did you feed it through Mummy's bellybutton????'

'Mummy fed it through a special tube inside her. That's why she's been eating a little more.'

'A tube inside her?!? A tyre tube!!?!'

'No, just a tube that grows in mummies when they're having babies.'

I didn't know what to say, so I burst out crying and said that I wanted my breakfast and that the baby better not try to get into my tummy. Or even into inside next to it.

'After breakfast well go and see Mum, and if you're a very good girl we'll let you see your new brother.'

I didn't want to go, but when you're four you have to do whatever your Mum or Dad say or you get carried out of the house anyway.

We walked down the hill and over the little wooden bridge, up the track past Scratcher's place, and down the path into the Base Hospital. A magpie was chortling up on the roof, but he didn't have a new brother to worry about, and even if he did have he could always fly away and live somewhere else. A few blowflies were buzzing around the front door of the hospital – in a country town bad news travels pretty fast. Dad and I and the flies went inside and down the passage, funny smells creeping up my nose and squawks coming from somewhere.

'That'll be him.'

Dad turned into a door and there was Mum, lying back in a great white bed, with spears of red and yellow flowers in a jug next to her.

'Hello, darling,' Mum said. I wasn't at all sure about this because she usually only said darling when I was in trouble.

'I've brought you some peanuts, Mummy.' I nearly called her 'elephant'.

'That's very thoughtful of you,' she said, but she didn't look all that interested in them.

'When are you coming home, Mummy? I want some breakfast."

'Daddy will get you your breakfast.'

I looked at Dad. I think that he thought that he could cook. He was always boasting about it, but my toast that morning had made my teeth go black and I'd had to brush them for ages.

'Mummy will be in hospital for ten days. Then she'll come home if she's feeling all right.'

When you're four you don't know much about ten days, but I noticed that Dad had only said that Mum'd be coming home. They must've decided to leave the baby at the hospital.

'Come on, we'll go and see baby brother.'

Dad seemed to puff up whenever he said 'brother'.

'I'll just look at the flowers, Daddy. You get me when you've finished.'

Dad picked me up and carried me out of the room. He walked down the passage the other way and stopped outside a window. This was the first time that I'd ever seen a window inside a place. Behind it was a smiling nurse, holding up a bundle with a red face or something.

'There he is! There's your new little brother!' Dad puffed up again. 'We've decided to call him William. Isn't he terrific!'

'Can I go back and look at the flowers now?'

****

He sat in his high chair, head thrown back like a rabbit sniffing the air for ferrets, mashed pumpkin squeezing between his fingers on to Brissy's head, peas rolling all over the tray and in his hair, gravy dripping between his toes, and the back of his nappy bulging with something which I hadn't really got used to, yet. He yelled and laughed as he threw a dollop of potato into the fire and dropped his bottle onto the passing cat.

It was teatime at Pendles'.

Not that it was different from any other meal, except for the ingredients making up the recipe. Sometimes it was porridge falling on to the dog. Sometimes Weeties and Vegemite, sometimes stewed apples or pears or rhubarb. Always a disgusting mess. No one seemed to mind, except me. Mum kept on putting more food in front of him, the cat learnt to walk further and further away, Brissy licked up whatever fell on her and got fat, and Dad just puffed up.

No one took any notice of me.

It'd been like that almost from the start. A couple of days after William had arrived at the hospital out of next-to Mum's tummy Nan came up from Melbourne to stay, to look after us. The toast suddenly got better but I had to brush my teeth three times a day, even when I hadn't been eating lollies. Every day we went to see Mum, the worst time being when we met Scratcher on the way.

'Where're you going, Lissie?'

'No where, really.'

'Why's your Dad going no where, too, Liss?'

'He isn't, Scratcher, he's going some where.'

'Where's he going, then?'

'He's only going down to the Base.'

'What's he going there for? Has he cut his thumb or something?'

'He's a doctor.'

'Doctors shouldn't get sick.'

'He's not sick. And why shouldn't he get sick if he wants to? It's only mothers who aren't allowed to get sick. You're father gets sick often enough.' I'd got him there.

'That's only the day after payday. It's the worry of having all that money. The rest of the time he's all right. Unless he doesn't want to go to work.'

He threw a stone at a magpie and I started to walk on.

'Why's he going to hospital if he's not sick and he hasn't cut his thumb?'

He never gives up. It wasn't till years later that he turned into a funny kid.

'He's going to see Mum.'

'What's he going *that* way for, then? You live back there.'

'She's down at the Base.'

'Oh....has *she* cut her thumb?'

Dad and Nan were out of sight.

'No! She's had a baby!' I yelled and raced off.

When we came out of the hospital later Scratcher was out the front. So was Jingo. So were David and Craig and

Ray and Alex, and Lone and Robbie and Gravyhead. And the McPhees with the wind blowing towards us.

I ducked behind Dad and scurried home, face pink and hot. Why'd Scratcher told Jingo? Why did they all just look at me, not saying anything? It wasn't my baby. I didn't want it. Nobody'd even asked me whether I needed it around.

Every day when we went to see Mum they were waiting afterwards, never saying anything, and when Mum finally came home they all walked along behind, right up to our front gate. I'd never been so embarrassed.

Luckily that was the day I started school. Dad took me up, after Nan had cut my lunch and got my school bag ready. I had a jam sandwich, a bunch of grapes, and a bottle of lemon cordial. Dad left me at the front door of the Infant School and went off, in a bit of a hurry I thought. He didn't seem to want to stay to meet my new teacher, so I went in and looked for my peg, to see if I had my name on it.

***

'Pendle, is it!'

A voice boomed behind me and my bag fell off its hook. What was it? I turned around and stared into a mountain covered with daisies and strawberries.

'Come here, girl!'

I didn't know what to do. I was already in the foothills, with a huge overhang blocking out most of the light.

'That's it! Well done! I knew we'd get along well together!'

The rest of the light went out and I was lifted into the air, trying to find something to breathe.

'I'm Mrs Phelpps!'

I was done for, if I couldn't get air.

Suddenly there was light again, and air, and birds were singing in the world outside.

'Mrs Phelpps! Thank you very much for letting me go!" I put an extra inverted comma in there so that you'd know that I really meant what I said.

'Go into the room and sit on the mat, child!'

Behind me was a doorway into a room; in front of me was Mrs Phelpps. I went behind me.

There were little tables in there, stretching across the room in rows. Across the front wall hung a long blackboard with big letters and little letters chalked across the top. A piano stood in the far corner, next to a table as big as a house. Beside the door was an iron stove, so that the heat could go outside in the winter.

Between the blackboard and the little tables and the piano and the stove were the mats, and on the mats was a boy: Jingo. He looked at me and I looked at him.

'Sit down, dear!'

I sat on the mat nearest the door. Jingo was on the one farthest from the door. We both looked at our knuckles. Slowly the mats filled up, with children blown in by Mrs Phelpps.

I didn't hear any mothers or fathers, and forgot all about babies and little brothers. He wasn't a little brother you'd, anyway, and the Infant Room roof was a very long way above my head. The day I'd been waiting for had begun.

'Now, children. Form two lines, boys on one side and girls on the other, holding hands. No, not that way children, this way. THIS way! That's right. No, you! THIS·WAY!! You don t hold hands that way. THIS way! That's right. No, you! THIS WAY!! Now face this way. That's right. No! You! THIS WAY!! Now walk to the door that way. THIS way! Yes, yes, you! I said THIS way, through the door. No, no. Open the door first! That's right! Now go through the doorway. Good. No, not that way! THAT way! THAT WAY YOU!! Keep together. No! Stay in your lines! YOUR LINES! Come along. No, not so quickly. YOU! Come back here! It's not time to go home yet! Good girls. Boys! Don't let go of the girls' hands! YOU! I said don't let go of the girls' hands! No, don't try to hold ALL of the girls' hands! Only the girl next to you! No, not that one! She's already holding someone's hand! The one next to her. That's a boy! Hold that one's hand! Good. Now down the steps. Stop pushing the girls! You! I said stop pushing the girls! DON'T LET GO OF HER HAND! That's right. Good, good. Over towards the pole. Keep holding hands. Good. That's better. Not so slow back there. Keep up. Not you! You slow down! Good, good, now we're getting there. Keep those lines straight. STRAIGHT! Yes. March in step, now. Not back to the step! One two one two. Stop. I said stop! STOP! Don't bang into each other! STOP STILL! Keep in line! Hold hands still! Stop holding hands! Let go of each other's hands! You may STOP HOLDING HANDS NOW! PENDLE! let go of that boy's hand! YOU!! Oh...good morning, Mr Braden!'

'Good morning, Mrs Phelpps. We've been waiting for you: for some time. Did you forget: that we have assembly every: morning? Especially on the first day: back. My class has been standing: here for at least two minutes. Please get your kiddies here: promptly tomorrow.'

'Yes, Mr Braden. It was just that I was having a little trouble with one of the new boys.'

'Oh?! Which one, Mrs Phelpps? Please ask him to: come out here so that I can, ah, meet him.'

Mrs Phelpps dragged out someone who was probably someone's little brother but who didn't think he was quite little enough. His feet didn't touch the gravel as he went to meet Mr Braden.

'So this is the little: trouble-maker!' Mr Braden cuffed him on the ear. 'See that you behave: yourself in future! Get back into line. I don't want to have to: meet you again!'

But he did, almost every day for the next six years, and quite often a few of us went with him.

We saluted the flag and sang God save somebody for some reason and stumbled back into the Infant Room and had a drink of milk and finally went home.

3

Train

...where we start going on our holiday.

Two cats silently appeared in the back garden. I didn't know where they'd come from – I'd never seen either before. One was ginger and white, with a few black patches, and the other was mainly a colour that's not in the books – ginger waves through black hair, making it look like a fire that's just about burnt out. They were probably sisters.

At first they didn't see me, as I was sitting very still on the verandah, then one of them turned its head and caught sight of me, and stared, its tail stretched out behind it like a hairy hiccup.

The other remained ignorant, rubbing its head against the ashy one's cheek. Then it saw me, too, and stared, whilst the other rolled onto its back and sunned its tummy.

I didn't like cats so I stamped my feet on the boards and hissed 'Scat cats!' They stood slowly, arched their backs a little rudely, and sauntered off under the fence, bare bottoms showing what they thought of me.

How do cats get away with it? If I'd done that I would have needed more than a fence to save me from whichever grown-up was around at the time. Cats are like boys – they have their own rules.

I suppose that by now you've noticed that 'scat' is only 'cats' spelt differently, so that was the right word to send them on their way, but cats are too dumb to appreciate good words. Quite a few words are like that: you can mix them up and get other words out of them. I think these kinds of words are called anachronisms or something. I wish you could mix cats up like that and get different animals, or, better still, boys. I'd make a Jingo!

I liked sitting on our back verandah, especially in the afternoon, when the sun started to move over behind the hill, making the trees disappear in their own shadows. Sometimes, when the wind was blowing up the hill, the clouds' shadows seemed to be racing up to attack the big shadow coming down from the trees, but the big shadow always won because the sun went down.

'Well, Liss,' I said to myself, 'it's time to get cracking. Stop being a lazy crazy and start packing.'

The next day we were off on a holiday, our first one away from Niamong. Actually Mum and Dad had had a few holidays away from Niamong, but that was before I was born so they didn't count. And they only went on their own, too, together; this time it'd be the four of us, which made it a proper family holiday.

We had to get up to Ballargo by three o'clock in the morning to catch the train across to Bunneroo where Granddad lived. Mr Proudlove was going to drive us up in his car, and he was going to collect us at midnight.

Inside the house it was cool and dark after the sunny verandah, the warmth turning into coolth. My bedroom was on the right, opposite Bill's room and next to the spare room. My window stretched from floor to ceiling, and if I wanted to I could open the bottom part and walk out onto the side verandah and look at the main road and the railway crossing. I could have seen the trestle bridge, too, if a hill hadn't been in the way. In the winter it was best as Dad sometimes lit a fire in the old fireplace, and the flickering flames made the inside of my eyelids go redder and the crackling, burning wood sent me off to sleep, and the fire kept my nose warm.

Everything was ready on my bed, the suitcase was on the floor, and the things on the bed wanted to get into the case so they could have a holiday, too, so I helped them out by helping them in. It only took five minutes sitting on the lid to shut the case, and then Mum called me for tea.

I wished she hadn't. Bill was impossible; he was so annoying that I could hardly stand him, even sitting down. He kept running round the table, dropping bits of bread and jam on the carpet and crowing and getting more food and dropping that and knocking my arm that was holding a drink of milk which went all over my dress so I had to leave the table to change and by the time I came back my chops were cold and Brissy had come into the dining room to lick up the rubbish dump and get fatter.

Why do little boys have to get so excited when they're going somewhere? Going off with Bill was the same as Guy Fawkes night, or the fourth of July – explosions everywhere – and that was before we'd even started.

After tea we were going to go to bed for a while, and Mum was going to wake us up at half past eleven.

Bill certainly wouldn't go to sleep and I didn't think that I would, either, but there was nothing else to do. I lay down under the eiderdown in my travelling clothes and looked at the patterns on the ceiling. Mum was playing the piano quietly in the lounge. Dad was in the kitchen making a cup of tea. Somewhere up the valley a boobook owl was booing a book in an owlish sort of way, trying to frighten a mouse out into the open.

'Wake up, sleepy bags! Time to go!' Dad had on his warm coat and was carrying a torch. 'Mr Proudlove'll be here in a few minutes!'

I stumbled out into the passage. Our four suitcases stood beside the front door, travelling rugs folded over them so that they looked like Shetland ponies waiting for their oats on a cold night.

Mum came out of Bill's room, carrying him, asleep, with his head on her shoulder. He didn't look too bad that way, but before I could start feeling soft-hearted a car crunched up the drive and stopped outside, which was the best place for it to stop as there wasn't all that much room in the passage with the cases and us.

Outside was so big. And quiet. The sky was huge and I could almost see for miles, except that it was dark as dark on the ground. There was no world, only sky and stars, and Dad holding my hand as we walked down the steps to the car.

'Hello, John. You're right on time.'

'Good evening, Dr Pendle. Mrs Pendle. How are you, Liss?'

'It's a lovely night, Mr Proudlove.'

'Bonzer. The best this year, Mrs Pendle. We'll have no trouble getting to Ballargo tonight.'

Mr Proudlove tied our cases onto the rack at the back and we piled in, Dad in the front and Mum, Bill, and me in the back. I snuggled up to Mum's soft fur coat, Mr Proudlove cranked the car, and we set off down the drive.

Mum'd been home from hospital for about eight years that night so I didn't quite see why Bill should still be allowed to sleep with his head on her shoulder. She'd better watch out or she might find herself sitting in a puddle!

In a moment we were on the main road, turning across the railway line, and then heading up the hills towards Ballargo.

It's very difficult trying to keep snuggled into your mother at the same time as you're trying to look out the window at the night, especially when the car's bending around the hills and along gullies and drumming across wooden   bridges,,,and   your   eyelids spend,,,more..,.,and.,.,more.,,., time,,,,,,trying to reach the floor,.,.,.,and so you go to   sleep.

I woke up when Mr Proudlove stopped the car at Ballargo station, his headlights almost drowning out the bare globes over the ticket window. We were at the back of the station, really, the part where people parked their cars and carts, and trucks stopped to pick up goods for the shops in the town, which was just back up the road a bit. Ballargo was a lot bigger than Niamong so the station was much larger than ours, too. It almost looked like an old house.

Dad bought the tickets for Bunneroo while Mr Proudlove carried the suitcases around to the goods office to be put in the guard's van when the train arrived. Bill had woken up, too, by this time and he was looking around as though he'd been swallowed by a whale.

'Where's the train, Mum?'

'It hasn't arrived yet, son.'

'Why isn't it here, Mum?'

'It's not due for a few minutes.'

'What do we want dew for, Mum?'

'Not 'dew,' 'due,' son. The time it's supposed to get here.'

'What time's it s'posed to get here, Mum??'

'A quarter to three, Billy.'

'Have we had breakfast yet, Mum?'

'No, it's not time for breakfast, Bill.'

'When'll we have breakfast, Mum?'

'At BREAKFAST TIME!'

'Mum? Mum! Where'll we have breakfast?'

'On the train!'

'Mum. What'll we have for breakfast?'

'William!'

We thanked Mr Proudlove for bringing us and walked through the gate onto the platform. Down towards one end of the platform there was a light on a thin lamppost, with millions of bugs flying around it. At the other end was another post, but no light, and I don't know whether there were any flying bugs up there or not. If there were any they must've been a pretty dim lot, crashing into each other all over the place.

The station was great. It had iron posts holding up the verandah roof, and lots of doors. As we walked along I saw that the first one was the Station Master's office. He wasn't t here that night; he was probably home in bed. I knew this because the man inside had 'Assistant Station Master' on his cap, and he was much younger than a proper Station Master would be.

The next door was shut, but I could see through the window that it was a sort of kitchen. Dad knocked on the door and waved at one of the ladies inside. He must've known her. She came over and opened the door, washing a tea-ey smell all over us.

'Yes? What is it?'

'Could we have a cup of tea, please?' asked Dad. I thought he sounded a bit quiet.

'It's not time yet.'

'We would really love a cup of tea, please. If it's not too much trouble.'

'It's not time yet.'

'We've come from Niamong . . .'

It looked as though we were going to get in when he said that. She opened the door a little and we moved towards her.

'It's not time yet. I'm sorry'. And the door closed.

'I hope she never needs a doctor on time,' muttered Dad.

'There it is! There it is!' yelled Bill, and Dad stopped starting to get angry.

Up the track we saw a light waving up and down, then a loud whistle blew.

The kitchen door opened. We tried to go in but Bill was pulling all of us at once the other way to see the train come in and in a second or two he'd nearly pushed us off the edge of the platform.

The great engine, black and hissing like a cloud of angry snakes, clanked and spat into the station, the engine driver leaning out to see whether Bill was going to jump onto the rails in front of him.

The engine hissed more and there was a lot of squealing from the wheels (which reminded me of the day the pigs got loose in Niamong) and the train stopped.

Most of the doors opened and people climbed down onto the platform and went into the tearoom, or into one of the other rooms, or went for a walk up the platform. It looked as though most were trying to get a drink or something to eat, jamming through the doorway, pushing and shoving, spilling things, dropping money on the floor, and bursting out again into the night.

'All aboard!'

The Assistant Station Master officialled out of his office and began ringing his bell.

Everyone rushed for the train as the engine driver blew his whistle. The tearoom ladies pushed an old chap out of their doorway and locked the door.

We climbed up onto the step and into the carriage. Our compartment was about halfway down and we had it all to ourselves. We sat down on lovely leather seats, Bill and me on the window side so that we could look out.

'Mum, I want to go to the toilet.'

'In a minute.'

'I can't wait.'

'You can't go just yet.'

'I need to go!'

'Just hold on a minute.'

'It's coming!'

'Put a cork in it!' yelled Dad.

'I'll try.'

Bill started mumbling to himself, and I won't tell you where he was holding himself – boys're disgusting things.

The guard blew his whistle and the engine driver blew his whistle and I think I heard Bill whistling and the train shuddered and we were off.

'Mum!!'

They should've called him 'bladdermouth'.

'All right. I think we're far enough out now.'

Mum and Bill went out into the corridor as the train started to get up speed. I thought that since they were going I might as well, too, so I left Dad and followed.

The train was rocking from side to side, making me bump against the walls, but it was fun. Mum was up the other end of the carriage, pushing Bill through a door.

'Is there only one, Mum?'

'Yes dear. One in each carriage.'

'Why did we have to wait for the train to get going?'

'I thought that you'd all like to see us pull out of the station.'

A minute or so passed and then the door burst open. Bill fell into the corridor, his pants around his ankles.

'Liss! Liss! Mum! Dad! You should see where it goes!'

'Yes, yes, dear. That's enough. Pull your pants up.'

'But Mum, it goes...'

'I know, dear, now get your pants up and go back to Dad.'

'But...'

'Your turn, Liss,' and I was shoved into a box and nearly fell down the toilet. It was a cubby hole! Lucky Bill had had to sit down. If he'd had to stand up, with the train rocking all over the place, anything could have happened...

I pressed the button and went back to our compartment.

'Did you see it, Liss?! Did you see it?!'

'What?' I'd sat straight down, so I hadn't seen much.

'Where it went?!?'

'That's enough, William. Be quiet and settle down.'

'But...'

'William!'

When Mum turned away he looked at me and pointed downwards. I couldn't see anything interesting there, so I looked out the window at the night...

***

'The sun's coming up, sleepy bags!'

I'd done it again!

Outside the clacketing train the paddocks were starting to turn yellow, the black patches shrinking as the sun crept up. I couldn't see the sun rise because we were heading straight into it, but it didn't really matter. It was terrific looking out the window, watching the cattle and sheep run away from the engine, and bits of smoke wisp past as we rushed down the hills that seemed to be growing bigger.

'Mum, is it time for breakfast yet?'

It was Stomach talking, again.

'What do you think, dear?'

Dad looked at his watch. He'd just about stopped puffing up whenever he looked at Bill nowadays, thank goodness

'It's nearly seven o'clock – I think they might be open. Come on.'

Bill leapt up and disappeared out the door.

'Not that way. This way, feller.'

He was half way to the toilet.

'But I want to go.'

'Oh. All right.'

So we waited outside for ten minutes while the train rocked and Bill did whatever he was supposed to have wanted to do.

When he finally came out he whispered in my ear.

'I don't believe you,' I said. 'You're lying again.'

'I'm not! It does! Go and have a look!'

'Mum. I think I'll go, too, while we're here.'

She looked at me a bit.

'Well hurry up, or breakfast will be off.'

It was just as well that I didn't really want to go, because when I went in and looked I was so embarrassed. It did! I quickly put the lid down and went out.

'You didn't take long! Come on.'

Bill looked at me, grinning all over his face and neck, but I didn't look at him. I was pink. How could they do that?! What if someone was walking along the line! I wondered if Mum knew? What if Dad found out? I wasn't going to go in there again. But Bill did. Every ten minutes, and I think he went into every one on the train.

Breakfast was in the buffet car, and that was the right name for it. We got buffeted around all the time, especially when we went around bends, and the cutlery kept sliding all over the table. But I didn't mind because it was the first time that I'd ever been waited on. A man in a white coat took our order for toast and a glass of milk, and bacon and eggs for Dad and Bill, and Weeties before the bacon and eggs for Bill. And an extra glass of milk. We sat for a little while after we'd finished, looking out the window at the hills and trees, while Bill had some more toast, and then we went back to the compartment.

Well, we didn't exactly go right back because we decided to stop for a while where the two carriages joined together. This was the best place on the train, much better than the toilet, and even Bill thought so.

At the end of each carriage was a little metal platform, with gates at each end and fences across the sides. A metal flap went across the space from one carriage nearly to the other and lay on top of another flap on the other side. This was where you walked from carriage to carriage, or you could just stand on it and get shaken backwards and forwards and get frightened of falling off. Dad said it was quite safe as long as you didn't do anything silly. He looked at Bill when he said that.

After a while Mum and Dad went back to the compartment and left us. They didn't like getting soot in their eyes all the time, but that didn't worry me. After all, there was just a chance that Bill would do something silly, and fall off the train.

4

Holiday

...where we all get a terrible fright.

We were still on the train's platform between the carriages when the train started to slow down for Bunneroo Siding. For ages and ages we'd been playing pirates and Indians and cops and robbers and bushrangers attacking the mail train with millions of dollars of gold bars to be stolen or protected. Bill would be on one side of the platform and I'd be on the other. We'd close the gates between the platforms and fire at each other and melt into the shadows when passengers wanted to cross, and then shoot them in the back as they went through the door. We must've frightened a million sheep beside the line and the crows and kookaburras disappeared in a great hurry.

I didn't really enjoy all this as I was getting a bit old for it, but it kept Bill out of Mum's hair for a long time and that meant that I might be able to get into it on my own later.

The Siding was a kind of railway station that wasn't a railway station. Trains only stopped there if someone was getting off, or had to be picked up, or if a farmer had an especially big mob of sheep to send over to Ballargo. I don't know why it was called a siding – trains never went into it sideways. It should really have been called a fronting, or even a backing, or else they should've made trains with wheels that could turn like a car's.

Granddad was waiting at the siding, leaning on the roof of his old ute with his face hidden in the shade of a hat the size of Old Mary's saddle. We all piled off the train and into Granddad and watched the train chuff off up the valley towards wherever it was going.

'Hiya Liss! How's my girl! Hello there, King Billy! I suppose there're no bushrangers left alive down the track!? G'day kids! Have a good trip?'

Granddad always called Mum and Dad 'kids,' which either meant that he'd forgotten how old they were or else he thought they were young goats. Anyone could see that they were nearly as old as the hills so he must've been calling them goats, but they didn't seem to mind.

'Kids' is another one of those words I was telling you about before: put the 's' in front instead of at the end and you've got 'skid,' which is what you do when goats are around and you don't watch where you're walking.

Granddad's ute wasn't very big, and it wasn't like the ones they have nowadays. He said it was the only one that he could afford, and that was the make of car it was, too a Ford. He called it his Old Tin Can, and when it broke down he called it the Tin Can't. (Granddad's jokes were as bad as Dad's, but with Granddad it was all right: you didn't have to put up with them all the time, pretending to laugh. Little brothers are even worse because they hear their fathers cracking weakies and they try to do the same and keep yelling at you, 'Get it? Get it?' You get it all right – in the neck.)

Mum got in the front with Granddad, and Dad and Bill and I got in the back – the best place. At the very back was a flap which opened downwards, so that awkward, heavy loads could be lifted in and dumped on the floor, like our suitcases. On each side were wooden benches, and these were mainly to sit on, although one or two other things were stuck onto them so we had to be a little careful where we sat – at night Granddad left the ute under a tree, and the birds that slept there didn't only sleep there.

When the engine was going it chugged and made little noises out of its bottom, but I tried not to listen to those or look at Bill when it happened.

We drove into town and stopped at the General Store to collect our supplies for the week, and for Granddad to fill up with petrol. Bunneroo was always called 'town' by everybody who lived anywhere near it but for us Niamongites it was very small stuff. It only had the store where we stopped (which was also the post office and bank and greengrocer), and a pub that was more like a shack. It didn't even have any robbers or murderers because there wasn't a police station.

But the gravel main street was wider than any of ours, and dustier.

Although we'd only been driving for about three minutes from the siding we all felt like a rest so we all went into the shop to help Mum buy the provisions.

'Mum, can I have one of those?'

'Would you buy us one of those please Mum?'

'Can I have a packet of those please Mum? Mum?'

'Those are scrumptious, Mum, can we have a bag of those?!'

'Oh, look at those! Mum, you've got to buy us six of those!'

'Those are bigger than those, Mum, you only need to buy us four of those instead of six, Mum!'

'Mum. Mum. Mum! Can I have one of those toffee apples please Mum? Mum! Dad. Will you buy me one of those?'

'No.'

Bill's face started to rain then so we took our stuff and put it in the back of the ute and watched the shopkeeper fill us up with petrol.

We weren't going to stay at Granddad's this time: we were going up to the house he'd built when he and Grandmother were first married and started growing an apple and pear orchard. No one had been there for years but he said it was still in good condition and would keep out the rain, if there was any. He'd been up the previous day and given it a good clean out (Mum looked a bit doubtful when he said this) and taken up some pots and pans and things.

In no time at all we'd left town and were driving through the dust into the hills. The road was quite curvy, with lots of tree ferns on either side, so that we seemed to be bumping along on the back of a large green and brown caterpillar, and each little valley we passed had a dam across it. One or two of these had brown ducks floating on them, and Bill spent his time trying to count more windmills on his side than I counted on mine.

He won easily because there weren't any on my side, except for one that had no vanes on it and the water tank beneath it had fallen on its side, rusting in the long grass.

Huge trees spread their branches across the road, which was the stoniest one I'd ever seen. All the time stones kept thumping up and hitting me on the bottom, or that was what it felt like. Bill was laughing so much that his face nearly fell off.

That was always happening. He got really bad when he started school. All the time he aggravated me, spying on me, putting things in my bed and down my blouse. Once he changed my jam sandwich into a lizard and another time he put tadpoles in my drink bottle.

The best part about sitting in the back of the ute was that it was almost impossible to hear what he was saying, so all I had to put up with was looking at what he was doing or trying to do. I could see that he was pretending to drive the ute this time. He'd never forgotten when Dad had sat him on his knee just after he'd bought his new car. It wasn't quite a new car, but it was new to us, and we'd only ever sat in the back up till then.

I'd asked Dad if I could have a drive and the world splashed all the colours of the rainbow when he said that I could. He sat me on his knee, put the car into first gear, and away I steered. Round the top of the drive, dipping a little into the gutter, and then down the hill to the gate, with Bill jumping up and down on the back seat. I could hardly concentrate.

'Can I have a go, Dad?! Can I have a go? I want a drive, too, Dad! It's not fair if she gets a go and I don't! Hurry up and stop, Liss, I'm going to have a drive! It's my turn, now. Get out, Liss! There's the gate! Stop the car! Come on! Dad!'

There was no way that Dad would give him a go: he was too small and, besides, I'd had to wait all these years so why shouldn't he?

'All right,' said Dad, puffing up a little at the idea of his son driving a car at his age. It made me sick.

The door was wrenched open and I found myself tugged off Dad's lap and dropped on to the drive.

Bill jumped over me, showering me with gravel, and crashed onto Dad in the wrong place. Dad gave a little yell and looked all over the sky for a few moments, some of the puff gone out of his face, which looked a little white.

'Come on, Dad, get going! Put your foot down on the exciterator!'

'Just a minute, son, I've got to get my breath ba...I mean I've got to turn the car around first.'

Backwards and forwards we went until the car was pointing up the hill towards the house.

'Ready, son?'

Every time he said that I wondered why he didn't call me 'moon'.

The car went everywhere except off the drive. We went along the left hand gutter, then the right, then back to the left again. I was almost seasick when we went around the curve outside our front door and then we started down the hill again, aiming at the gate like a cannon (the one that you have on men-o-war, not the kind that you have in church, although I wished we had one of them then!).

'Faster, Dad!' said the motoring master.

I suppose that Dad thought that he'd give Bill a bit of a fright so he pressed his foot straight to the floorboards. The car leapt forwards, throwing Bill off Dad's lap and under the steering wheel, which he was still hanging on to. The car slewed around to the side, lurched through Mum's best garden bed, and headed for the fence. Dad kept jamming his foot onto the brake to stop the car but that didn't do any good because Bill was in the way. This meant that Dad's foot kept kicking Bill in the stomach, which was full for once, or at least it was until it'd had enough of Dad's feet in it, when it emptied itself colourfully all over Dad's legs. The fence fell over itself trying to get out of the way and we charged through the paddock, finally splashing nose-first into the creek, back tyres fountaining black mud all over Brissy, who was sorry that she'd pounded out to see what was happening.

The fish kept away from the creek for weeks after that, I had a black eye till the end of the holidays, Brissy had a very long bath, Dad had to ask Mr Proudlove to drive him around a while, and Bill didn't even pretend to drive a car until we were heading up to Granddad's old house. He didn't think a great deal about food until the next day, either.

Granddad stopped the car outside the old house and we climbed out to look at it.

It was on the side of a hill. The front door opened off the drive, on the high side, with a tangle of old roses beside the path, mixed up with dandelions and thistles and various other weeds. Down both sides of the house were enormous pine trees. At the back, and stretching all the way to the forest, was a line of gum trees, smooth trunks looking like candles in the sun. Behind us, on the other side of the drive, were the old apple and pear trees, full of branches and covered in hairy green and grey stuff, which Granddad said was liken, but like what he didn't say.

Clouds covered the sun as we went inside, through the thick bluestone wall, into the kitchen. This was quite large. On the far wall were the wood stove and chimney, and wood box next to it. This was one of those good ones that had a door in it so that you could fill it from outside. When the others weren't looking I saw Bill climb through it and disappear outside. The rest of us walked around the house, looking at the two bedrooms, for Mum and Dad and Granddad, the sleepout, for Bill and me worse luck, and the sitting room. A wonky verandah clung to the back of the house, propped up on poles, and the laundry was underneath. Around the corner, in between the pine trees, was the toilet, but I wasn't too certain that I'd ever go in there.

By this time Mum'd decided to get the lunch ready. She seemed to be fairly happy with Granddad's cleaning-up and I knew she rather liked the wood stove — it was almost the same as ours at home. Dad set the table while Granddad lit the fire in the stove, and I cut some bread. We had some really interesting shapes that day, and different thicknesses, even in one slice, but I didn't think that anyone would mind.

There was a big table in the middle of the kitchen for our meals, wooden, with round, bulging legs. A bit like Mrs Phelpps's but not so dangerous. Cupboards were everywhere, mostly with old yellowed newspapers on their shelves.

'Lunch is ready, everybody.'

'I could eat a horse.'

'Don't say things like that, Granddad.'

'We don't have one, anyway.'

'Where's Bill?'

For once the Bottomless Pit wasn't there for a meal!

'I think I saw him go outside before.'

'Go and find him please Liss. And tell him to wash his hands!'

Why me!? I was starving, too, but *I* had to go out and find him. Why couldn't he find himself? Or, better still, why didn't he lose himself properly, for good?

'Bill! Where are you?'

I couldn't see him in the old orchard so I turned down the far side of the house.

'Bill! Bill!'

There was no sign of him on that side. I looked in the laundry, and down the hill towards the forest, but no sight. Then I heard him calling.

'Where are you?'

There wasn't much sun now and it was almost dark under the pine trees. I wasn't all that keen on the noise they were making when the wind breezed through them.

'Up here, Liss.'

He must be hiding in the toilet, with the redbacks. I opened the door carefully, which was a bit difficult as it was only hanging from one and a half hinges. Inside was almost dark. The seat went right across the back, with the lid in the middle, and cobwebs fell like white, sticky curtains from the roof. The place was full of everything I didn't like, except Bill.

I didn't shut the door: if any flies wanted to commit suicide in there they were welcome. Where could he be?

'Up here, Liss. Up here.'

I was already up here.

'No, not down there, up here!'

I went outside and looked up, and up. Up the groovy trunk of the great pine tree, up through the thick branches, up through the thinner branches, up to a dirty smudge near the top

'Lunch is ready,' I said, and went back inside.

I'd forgotten to tell him to wash his hands, but it wouldn't have made any difference. He says he never forgets, only that sometimes he takes a long time to remember something, especially washing his hands.

We'd just about finished our lunch when he finally came in, pine needles all over him so that he looked like a hungry spiny anteater. At home he was always filling slices of bread with whatever food was on the table – meat, potatoes, grapes, hardboiled eggs – and then stuffing them into his mouth. I'm sure that these mixtures always tasted the same, because everything in them fell out before he got them to his mouth. And old Brissy got fatter. Brissy wasn't having a holiday with us this time, but Bill still made his full-then-empty sandwiches.

After we'd cleaned up the mess, Bill and I went out to explore for the afternoon.

We went all over the place – through the orchard, around the dam, back down the track to the gate, right around the boundary fence, and into the forest – and didn't get back until nearly tea time.

Bill climbed the tree again.

In five minutes I was at the top, just below Bill's smelly feet, looking out over the trees and house. We could see right down the valley where the road went to Bunneroo. In the other direction a couple of crows were arking off to their sleeping tree, and right below me Dad was climbing the tree! I don't know why that surprised me, because he looked a bit like a tree himself. Once he told me that he was his school's champion high jumper, but I think that *he* was the high jump.

He looked around, trying to keep all the stuff Bill was scuffing down out of his eyes.

'I used to climb this when *I* was a boy!'

I hate it when parents go on like that, saying how different it was when they were young. I hate it, but I can't wait till I can say it to my own children.

'It might rain tonight,' said Dad, brushing away a cloud from his face. 'We'd better get down before it catches us up here. Tea's nearly ready, anyway.'

Granddad had lit the pressure lantern in the kitchen and it hissed its light all around the room, except under the table. The stove was burning warmly, cooking the chops and mashed potato and peas, and Mum was just rinsing the fruit under the tap. If we'd had more water she'd probably have given it a bath.

'What'll we do after tea, Mum?'

'Well, I think it's too dark for a walk tonight, and we'd likely get wet if we went too far.'

'Why don't we just sit in front of the fire and I'll tell you a story,' said Dad.

This was a new turn. Dad had never told a story in his life, if you don't count what he said to Mum after we drove the car into the creek that day.

'What sort of story?' Bill asked. 'I don't want anything about Goldilocks and the Three Wharves or anything.'

Bill wasn't too good on fairy stories: he liked blood and thunder.

'You'll find out, when I start.'

That meant that he hadn't a clue what he was going to say – he could go off anywhere and would probably get lost on the way. Still, it was worth a try, and he might surprise me again. After all, he *had* climbed up the tree.

Granddad and I did the dishes and tidied up the kitchen while Dad and Bill got the fire going in the sitting room. Mum went off somewhere else for a while and then we all turned up in the sitting room together.

The fire was burning strongly, lighting the room, making it feel warm and cosy. We didn't bring in the pressure lamp because that would have spoilt the story. Bright lights ruin a good story, so you either have to turn them off or make your mind go dark.

Mum sat in an old armchair by the fire and got out her knitting. Soon she was knitting away, her hands and needles jumping around like two pointy-beaked birds pretending to attack each other.

On the other side of the fire sat Granddad in a rocking chair, already nodding off to sleep. He must have heard Dad's stories before.

Bill and I were on a lumpy couch in the middle, where we got the best of the fire.

Dad sat between us and Granddad on an upright chair, not very comfortable but, then, he wasn't all that comfortable, either. We couldn't see him very well as he was a bit behind us, further away from the fire. I suppose he didn't need as much heat as we did, because he was so thin.

'Once upon a time,' began Dad.

Oh, no! How corny can you get!

'Once upon a time, in a land far away, there was a strange house.'

A goose bump jumped up on my left leg. That always happens when someone says something is strange.

'It was a very old house. It had a very tall, steep roof, with strange winged creatures crouched on each corner, staring out over the black mountains.'

The goose pimple turned into a flock of geese.

'A half-open door stood darkly between two huge open windows, making the house look like an evil giant, brooding in the night.'

A log fell off the fire, making me jump as a splatter of sparks rushed up the chimney. Granddad snored. I had two flocks of geese, all honking up my legs.

'Lightning flashed over the twisted chimneys, making them seem to leap over the roof.'

That was the third time Dad said 'over,' and I wished the story was over. It was giving me the creeps.

'Thunder growled threateningly in the valley and the wind whined eerily through the pine trees crowding round the strange house.'

The wind was whining through the pine trees outside *our* house! Bill picked up his old Shawl and held him so he could listen to the story, too.

'Down came the rain, lashing a lone horseman who appeared out of the dark forest. He was making for the old house, the *haunted* house!'

The hairs on my neck twanged up. Why hasn't someone put more wood on the fire? It was getting too dark in here

'Don't go there! lone horseman. Don't go there! Danger! Danger! But he kept on, doggedly. Or didn't he care?!'

I felt Bill cuddling into me. He was a good boy sometimes.

'Rain was dripping off the lone horseman, rivering down the lone horse's legs, blinding them both. But something seemed to be drawing them towards the door, that awful door.'

Why doesn't he turn away? I thought. Anyone could see that he'd get killed if he went into that dreadful place, full of ghosts and horrible dead monsters that come to life when the wind whines through the pines.

'On they went, closer, closer. The door creaked, opened a little. A loose shutter, unpainted all these years, banged and banged in the wind.

'The horse stopped, he could go no further: he *would* go no further. His keen senses had smelt the dreadful evil waiting, lurking inside.

'But the poor tired horseman knew nothing. He needed rest. Desperately he needed to put his head down and rest, safe from the horrors he'd been through.

'Wearily he fell off his faithful horse, dropping the reins to the untended path. He looked up, through the driving rain, and saw the door, beckoning him. Slowly he mounted the steps, not heeding his brave, exhausted horse's warning whinny behind him.'

I held Bill's hand, so that he wouldn't be frightened.

'One, two, three paces across the grey flagstones, slippery and wet. He reached out and pushed the door, stepping out of the rain, lightning blinding him as he stumbled into the blackness.'

YeoOWeRoFORTEEEHA-A-A!!!!

'Great Menzies Eyebrows!!' screamed Granddad, jumping out of his chair. What was that?!!'

'It sounded like a wild pig caught in a trap out there!' shouted Dad, his face white even with the red fire glowing on it.

WooOROWUNgRGHTLyA-A-A!!!

'It's not a wild pig! It's a black panther escaped from a circus!' yelled Granddad, knocking his chair over onto Dad's foot.

Bill had disappeared under Shawl, only his eyes peering through the holes, except that they were screwed tight shut. I bet he'd have to change his pants tonight. So would I.

AARGHwuglrAHRUMPHL!!!

'What is it?!' gasped Mum, who was scrabbling along the floor, tangled up in her knitting, which looked more like knotting.

'Come on. Granddad. We'd better go and see what it is!'

'Be careful! It might be dangerous!''

I wasn't going anywhere, and I think that Bill agreed with me for once.

Dad and Granddad rushed into the kitchen to get their torches and tore outside very slowly to see what was out there.

After a few minutes Dad came back, all in one piece as far as I could see.

'Where's Granddad?! What's happened to him??'

'Come out and see.'

This didn't seem like a good idea at all. If it'd got Granddad already why give it more people to eat?

'Come on. You should see this.'

GRUFFLWEeAaSNRgH!!

Bill and I looked at Dad from behind Mum and the knitting.

'Come on!'

Mum started to walk slowly outside. We went with her because it was better than being left behind.

Granddad wasn't eaten. He was standing under the big gum tree at the back of the house, just outside the living room, his torch shining up the trunk at one of the higher branches.

'There's your pig panther. Think he'll eat us?'

We looked up the beam of the two torches, trying to see what huge animal was crouching there, and we saw....a koala!!

A koala! All that noise and scaring from a koala! A cuddly, furry koala had almost frightened us all to death, even the grown-ups, and was going to make Mum do a bit more washing tomorrow.

He didn't make any more noise that night, probably being quite happy with his night's work, and we all went back inside for a nice hot cup of cocoa.

With the lamp lighting up the house properly.

5

Emperor Gum IV

...where we're all taken for a ride.

iamong was empty.

Everyone had gone, almost. Only the Post Office was open, and it was only open because it had to be. It might as well have been closed because Mr Armstrong was asleep on the counter, his left ear keeping cool in the wet sponge you use to save yourself the horrible taste you get when you lick envelopes. It would have needed quite a bit of stamping around to wake him up, but everyone had gone to the show.

All the shopkeepers had shut their shops in the main street and opened stalls at the Showgrounds. They said they did that to make the Show more interesting, but it was really so they could make more money. And I was going to help them.

The best part about the Niamong Show was that we didn't have to go to school, which meant that for one day of the year we didn't have *Show and Tell*.

Why do they have to have *Show and Tell?* Whenever you have something you really want to show you're not allowed to tell about it, and when you're bursting to tell about something you're told that you have to wait till it's your turn, which is always about three years away.

The trouble with school is a bit like the trouble with home – grown-ups make the rules, and they only make them up for children. Why doesn't Mr Braden have to sit at a small table all day, instead of prowling around all day frightening us all? Not that he frightens me all that much, or even anyone else, but he thinks he does, and that's the main thing.

Why doesn't Miss Hendley have to sit at a small table, too? Scratcher would know exactly which table *she* should sit at! And I'd make up my own sitting rule – I'd always sit next to Jingo, and help him with his work and give him a cuddle when he got it right. It would be a bit too much to ask that Mrs Phelpps should sit at a small table, because we'd soon run out of small tables. She could stand in the corner instead of Mr Phelpps for once.

Being in Niamong on Show Day was like being in a cowboy film, just before the showdown between the goodies and the baddies. About the only thing that you could see was a whole pile of nothing, but if you started walking down the street you were suddenly attacked by a fleet of flies – not the big blowies that came to the hospital the day Bill was born, but the little ones that get in your eyes and up your nose.

That's the really amazing thing about flies – it doesn't matter where you are or when you're there, as long as you're there, so are they. They must have scouts posted all the way along everywhere, just in case a human being should come along, and then they use the bush telegraph to let every other fly on the line know about lunch. How they can eat what they eat is beyond me. Sometimes I think they're even more disgusting than Bill.

I'd been saving my pocket money for weeks, ever since I realised that the Show was coming up. Mum and Dad always gave me some money for the Show, but never enough for me to buy what I needed to get as well as have the right number of rides on things. This year I was really going to have some good rides, so that was why I'd been saving my pocket money.

It was easy to tell where the Showgrounds were, because of the dust. There was nearly always dust in Niamong as there was nearly always a drought on, but at Show time there was more, with all the animals tramping and galloping round, and all the people walking around, and all the cars and utes churning up the gravel roads. The only ways to get rid of the dust were to have the wind blow it away, usually up your nose with the flies, or by it raining. It wasn't raining this time, and it wasn't winding, either, so there was dust.

Although it wasn't far to the Showgrounds from our house Dad had decided that we should drive, so that everyone would know that he had his car fixed after its time in the creek, and so they'd know that he could go out on more distant calls. I noticed people pointing and laughing as we drove into the car park – they must've been very pleased that Dad was on the road again.

We waited a minute for the dust to settle, then climbed out into the hot sun. Bill was already out, not worrying about the dust, leading the way to the turnstiles in a light brown cloud. Dad paid over the money to Mr Owen on the gate and we clanked through.

At last we could start spending and riding!

The Showgrounds was really one enormous oval, a white wooden fence separating the part that was meant to be grassy from the part that was where all the stalls and amusements were. It was all very flat except for the end opposite the gates, where there was a bit of a hill. A track went right round, so even Bill couldn't get lost, and if you started near the gate and walked around like a clock, ticking off the things you wanted to do and tocking to all your friends on the way, eventually you came back to the gate. This was called going clockwise, though why you should call a clock 'wise' I'll never know, as anyone can see that they haven't a brain in their heads and they go around in circles all day. The best clocks are grandfather and grandmother clocks, because they have Pendle-ums.

We decided to go clockwise and set off to the left, past the hot dog stall.

'Mum, I'm hungry.'

You know who that was. We'd just finished breakfast five minutes ago and Billious was ready to start again.

'Mum, can I have a hot dog?'

He loved saying 'hot dog,' because it sounded so funny. He didn't know why they were called that, and I wasn't going to tell him. Mainly because I didn't know, either.

72

'Bill, we've only just started! You'll run out of stomach before we're half way through!'

I thought Mum was a bit wrong, there. Last time when I made a marble cake – one of those pink, green, and yellow ones with the blue icing – I made the icing too runny and it dripped off the cake in a round circle on the bench, Bill ate all the cake and licked up the icing from the bench, and then he had tea. I didn't think he'd run out of stomach today.

'No I won't. I've got plenty left from breakfast.'

He had, too. He hadn't filled up his legs, yet.

'Well, all right. You've got your money. But only one…'

'*My* money?! I don't want to use *my* money, Mum.'

People started to push past us as we were blocking the way.

'Well, I'm sorry, but that was the agreement.'

'Mum, then I won't have any left for the rides or fairy floss!'

'You don't believe in fairies!' I said that to get him going, because I'd seen a couple of girls from his grade coming along, and he was pretty keen on them, even though he said he wasn't.

'Who'd want to believe in fairies!' he yelled. 'Only soppy girls believe in fairies!' he shouted, into his girlfriends' faces.

He was so embarrassed! For once I'd made *him* pink! And red and purple. The girls went off without saying anything to him, only smiling at Dad because he'd borned them when they were babies.

Walking around with Dad could be quite interesting, because nearly all my friends had been borned by him. In fact, nearly everybody that I *knew* had been borned by him, as long as they were round about younger than I was, so Dad knew a lot of people from when they were very young. They knew him from the same time, too, but they never remembered when they'd first met him. Still, they usually said hello to him, or smiled at him, or sometimes went a little red.

The mothers were really the funny ones, though. They generally looked somewhere else when they said hello to him.

'Mind out, Liss!' Dad called, and pushed me to the side as a horse was led past us. It clopped away and I could see it doing something that reminded me of a story Mum and Dad used to read to me, called Winnie the something or other.

Yes, mothers were funny: you could never work out what they'd do when they met Dad in the street. If he was on his own they'd stop and have a chat about things and their kids, Dad always asking about whichever ones of them he'd borned, and then they'd go off, with a bit of a pleased look on their faces. If I was with Dad when he met one of his mothers it wasn't quite the same. She'd say hello nicely to him, with a bit left over for me sometimes, and then she'd say a few things about the weather or not and then go on fairly soon. But if Mum was there they'd say 'Good morning, Dr Pendle. Good morning, Mrs Pendle' and walk quickly on, and I was sure that they were blushing as much as I do when something rude happens when Bill's around.

Other grown-ups are even more difficult to understand than your parents.

I shouldn't really be talking about babies being borned, you know. The proper word is 'delivered,' but when it's happening the baby is being born so after it's all over and it's cleaned up and the mother has finished her puffing and the father has started *his* puffing (if it's a boy), the borning is finished and it should be called 'borned'. That's what I think, anyway.

I could see that inside Bill's head there was a lot of thinking going on. How was he going to make it up with the girls, so that they'd think he was terrific again? How was he going to get his own back on me for setting him up? How was he going to get someone else to pay for his fairy floss? He was still a bit young to know how to work parents properly, although he usually got what he wanted without too much trouble. What he should have done was to wait until either Mum or Dad offered him something, and then made more of the offer by bargaining up or asking for something much more expensive that he didn't want anyway. Parents always get tricked like that and life is much more enjoyable for everyone.

'G'day, Mrs Pendle. G'day, Dr Pendle. Hiya, Liss.' It was Jingo! He was at the Show, all suntanned and clean, with only a few layers of dust on his shoes and legs.

'G'day, Dr Pendle. Hello, Mrs Pendle. How are ya, Liss.'

Jemmy came out from behind a tent, bits of straw hanging from his shirt.

'Howareyaallevrybody.'

It was Scratcher, covered in dust and one or two other things that told me he'd been somewhere near the sheep pens.

'Hello, boys,' said Dad, and Mum smiled at them a little nervously.

'Dad, can we get some drinks and hamburgers for us and the boys, please?' I asked, in my best doctor's daughter's voice. Jingo looked at me with admiration and Scratcher started to dribble a bit.

'For all of you!...er.....us?' said Dad, moving into the trap.

'Boy, it's really hot today, Mrs Pendle,' said Jingo, coming in on a flank. What a player!

'Well, er, what do you think, dear?' said Dad. I could almost feel the money in my hand.

'That's far too much,' said Mum, putting up the Traditional Mother's First Defensive Move.

'There are only seven of us,' I said, slipping in the classic Children's Stampede Parents Ploy.

Jingo threw out the Wallet Relief Pass: 'Maybe it's too hot for hamburgers.'

Dad caught the pass, relief spreading over his face.

'Here you are. Go and get some drink.'

'And some hot dogs and chips,' I put in, to finish him off.

'No! But you can have some fairy floss.'

Game, set, and match! Bill shrieked in ecstasy and amazement, and let me take the money for once without a fuss.

'If you get lost or anything, go to the police tent and they'll call us up,' said Mum, knowing what could happen when Bill and I went off with the others. Scratcher wasn't too keen on Mum saying 'police' and was already heading for the cold drink stall.

'You were great, Liss,' marvelled Jemmy.

'What skill!' chuckled Jingo.

'Drinks *and* fairy floss!' watered Scratcher.

'And they think *they*'re getting some, too!' said the walking stomach. 'How'd you do it, Liss?'

It was really tough listening to all these boys cheering me. I could hardly stay modest.

'Anybody could've done it,' I said, knowing that I was telling a lie, but they all knew that I was lying, and they all knew that I was supposed to lie because boasting wasn't appreciated all that much, which was something Bill hadn't quite cottoned on to yet.

'Besides, Jingo had helped a lot. It would've been much harder without him.'

We went over to Mrs Ray's lemonade stall and lined up along the counter. She had the best homemade lemonade in Niamong, but she only sold it at Show time. The rest of the year we had to work out all sorts of tricks if we wanted to get any, which was a pretty exhausting business.

At Show time, though, all you had to do was line up at the counter. And pay your money. Or, at least, your parent's money.

'Five lemonades please, Mrs Ray. Big ones. And cold ones.'

They were even colder than one of Mr Braden's frigidest stares, the ones he kept for Scratcher. We sucked the lovely tangy stuff up the paper straws, little pieces of lemon sticking in the tube sometimes so that you had to give an extra big suck, making a disgusting noise that no-one could tell you off for.

'Now what are we going to do?' asked Jemmy, after the last lusciously cool drops slid down our throats, turning the dust in our stomachs into mud.

'Why don't we go and have a look at the animals?' said Jingo. I thought that was a good idea, mainly because Jingo said it.

'What about the fairy floss?!' said you-know-who.

'We can get that on the way,' said Jingo. He was a born leader.

Most of the prize animals were up on the hill, on a flat piece of ground the other side of the road, so we went back in that direction. Mum and Dad had gone that way, too, but we made sure that we didn't catch up with them or let them see us. Jingo was right, of course, and we soon came to the fairy floss stall. Mrs Armstrong made the fairy floss every year. Mr Armstrong used to do it, but Mrs Armstrong discovered that he made most of it for himself and so they never made any money. He always said that he didn't eat it but no one believed him because there were always a dozen flies glued to his chin and cheeks, slowly turning pink as they flossed to death.

Dad used to say that you couldn't make something out of nothing, but with fairy floss you could certainly make nothing out of something. No sooner had you put a huge delicious frothy lump of it in your mouth than it disappeared into thin air, or fat stomach in Bill's case.

Where did it go? I didn't know. I just knew that another lump had to take its place, as quickly as possible.

From the top of the little hill we could see all of the Show Grounds, as well as a good deal of dust. To the right was where we'd come from and to the left was where we were going, after we'd looked at the animals. Behind were the animals we were going to look at before we went down to the left, for the rides. On the far side we could see the Ferris wheel, turning slowly around, the bottom part hidden by dust, the top in the clear, hot air. The McPhees thought that it was called a 'ferret' wheel, so they spent all their time on it. In fact the man in charge always turned the engine off when any McPhees were having a ride, because their smell spun the wheel faster than any engine could.

I loved the animals, and would have gone to see them even if Jingo hadn't suggested it. The babies were my favourites, especially the lambs and the calves and the chicks and the ducklings, but I liked the grown-ups, too.

All the judging had been done and the animals were covered with red, white, and blue ribbons, and blue, red, and white rosettes, and certificates were pinned to the posts, and proud owners were strutting about. It seemed that every animal had one some prize or other, and I supposed that they had to or their owners wouldn't be bothered bringing them again and what would a Show be without animals? They'd probably all get killed and made into chops instead, or chicken soup or something.

There seemed to be more dust than ever now and I wondered what was happening.

'Look!' cried Jingo. 'They're starting the Grand Parade!'

I always wondered how people managed to make some words start with capital letters when they said them. It's easy enough when you're writing a word to start it with a capital, but speaking capitals is quite different. Jingo was so clever.

The Marshall or Ringmaster or whatever he was called had opened the gate into the arena and the first animals were going in. These were the horses and ponies, followed by the sheep and a few goats. For some reason they didn't let pigs into the Grand Parade, but I think that was only since all those pigs got away when the train fell over. I don't know whether they were disgruntled about that, or gruntled, but as they didn't let hamsters go in either I didn't see why they should worry one way or the other. After all, pigs were only ham on the bone, and the longer they stayed away from showing themselves off the longer the ham would stay on the bone.

'Weeow!' called Scratcher. 'Look at that!'

We turned and saw Mr Bayly, but it wasn't him that Scratcher was wowing at. It was Mr Bayly's bull, a noble creature. But that wasn't really the right word for him because "noble" sounds like "no bull" and he was *some* bull! The boys walked around one side of him and I walked around the other side, and we met at the back after about ten minutes.

'Look at that!!' shouted Scratcher again, but when I looked at what he was pointing at I went bright pink and had to look away as quickly as I could.

'What do you think of him, kids?'

My face cooled down when Mr Bayly changed the subject.

'Isn't he a champion! In fact he's The Champion! He's The Champion Animal of the Niamong Show!'

I'd never heard anyone say so many capitals in one breath before.

'Look at that head!'

We couldn't have missed it in a dust storm.

'Look at those legs!'

They would've held up the trestle bridge, train and all.

'And what about that body!'

We couldn't think what, but we didn't have to for long.

'And look at that nose!'

That nose was lucky the McPhees weren't around or it would've been in trouble.

'And have you ever seen a ring like that!?'

Well, actually we had, but it was on Mrs Phelpps's wedding finger, almost hidden by the fat. Though it *was* the biggest one we'd ever seen through a bull's nose.

'Is he tame, Mr Bayly?' asked Jingo, who hadn't been on a farm very much.

'He's as tame as a kitten,' replied the proud buller.

I was quite pleased about that, because I hadn't been on a farm very much, either, especially one that had bulls running around it.

'As long as no-one pulls his tail,' added Mr Bayly.

We were so far from his tail down this end that we thought that was all right.

'Would you like a ride down to the arena, kids?'

One or two kids moved away from the bull a little.

'Emperor Gum IV wouldn't mind. He's as quiet as a lamb.'

Emperor Gum IV? What happened to Emperor Gum the III, II, and I? And why would you call a bull after a caterpillar?

'We called him Emperor Gum IV because he's as big as a king gum tree,' explained Mr Bayly, even though no one'd asked him. 'He was born on the 4th of July.'

'Why didn't you call him *Uncle Sam* then,' said Scratcher, and we all looked at him.

'Or the 'Star Spangled Hamburger,' said Bill, who always got his geography mixed up with his stomach.

'Righto, who's going up first?' asked Mr Bayly, ignoring all of these splendid suggestions. Grown-ups seemed to spend most of their lives asking children stupid questions.

'Ladies first!' I heard him say, and then I was doing the splits on top of a bristly mountain.

'Hold on to the halter, Liss.'

I held on to my halter neck but I couldn't see what good that was going to do.

'No, no. The one around EG's neck.'

Eg? Didn't that mean 'for example' or something?

Mr Bayly put a rope between my fingers and I hung on to it like a sparrow gripping a telephone wire in a hurricane.

'She's the bravest girl I know,' I heard Jingo say, and I nearly let go of the rope.

'Now the rest of you!'

And suddenly I had Jingo's arm around my waist! Tight!! Oh! Oh! First on the back of Old Mary, turtling through Jemmy's dam, and now on Emperor Gum IV, at the Niamong Show. The birds were singing in the trees and pretty little clouds were laughing merrily across a lovely blue sky and.......!!

We were off!

I heard a bellow of laughter behind me, getting further and further behind by the second. It sounded like the McPhees.

'Someone's pulled his tail!' screamed Jingo in my ear, through the rushing wind.

'Hold on for your life!!'

He should've said 'someones' with the little curly thing hanging in the air after the 's,' because it wasn't one who pulled the tail, but two, to get the bull really going, but now was no time to worry about spelling and things.

It was like being on top of a dragon just before it took off to devour a hundred maidens, except that it was the biggest bull in Niamong or anywhere else for that matter and it was charging down the hill with five of the best kids in Niamong on it who just wanted to finish their fairy floss. Straight through the Bowers' hot dog stall we crashed, giving Bill the chance to have one without paying for it at last. Straight through Mrs Ray's lemonade stall we crushed, cooling us all down for a second and making a lemon scented Emperor Gum, and us sticky all over.

The Ring Master leapt out of the way as the gate and fence broke. Out of the corner of my eye I saw the rest of the fence falling down right around the oval, like dominos on a table. We were on to the arena now, amongst all the other animals and their owners, when EG started really setting the example. Scratcher was the first to go, showing that he knew a little about diving as he disappeared over a horse which was starting to practise its hind-leg-walking trick. The other bulls broke away and galloped in all directions, most of them getting tangled up in horses' and ponies' reins as they joined in, too, showing off and prancing and generally looking for the whinnying line. I felt my dress beginning to rip then and I knew that

Jingo was about to go and look for Scratcher, which meant that Jemmy and Bill were already off somewhere. EG bucked his back and Jingo was gone and the noble creature and I were alone, except for the mess of people and animals spread out and running about and falling about and shouting and yelling and probably wetting their pants everywhere in front of us. EG didn't care about them and I wasn't all that concerned about them, either, just then. I now knew what Mum meant when she said she was at the end of her tether, but I'd never seen her with a bull at the other end!

I couldn't see anything. The dust from all the animals and shouting people blotted out the sun and we kept crashing into things and people and animals. EG started to sneeze as the dust billowed up his nose and I thought those hundred maidens had better watch out......when he skidded to a halt!!!

What'd happened?? Why'd he stopped?! How could he have stopped!! Nothing could have stopped that rampaging animal so quickly.

'Are you all right, Liss?!!'

It was Jemmy! He was holding the ring in EG's nose!!

'Yes, yes!' I lied, again. 'Yes. Thank you, Jemmy.'

'That's all right, Liss. I'm glad you stayed on! How'd you do it? You're amazing!'

The dust began to settle and I saw a huge ring of people standing round, looking at me, and not getting too close to EG. I patted his neck, to calm him down, and then Mr Bayly rushed over and lifted me off.

Just then Mum and Dad pushed through the mob and dashed up to me.

Mum spoke first.

'I thought I said to go to the police tent if you got lost!'

And then she disappeared me into her arms.

6

Dinner Time

...where it's very difficult.

S hould I tell Dad or shouldn't I?

Dads are pretty funny things sometimes. They're a bit like the word 'funny' itself. It can mean that you've just seen a great film at the flicks which made you roll in the aisle, or that you watched Scratcher crawling under the seats trying to pick up the Jaffas he'd dropped and which went skittering all over the place. Or it can mean that you think a person's crazy, like Scratcher when he stretched off the chewy stuck under the picture theatre seats and chewed it happily while Batman and Robin chewed up another bunch of evil criminals.

Funny is odd, amusing, strange, hilarious, queer, comical, puzzling, and.....funny.

You never know what Dads're going to do, or say. Sometimes they'll listen carefully when you're telling them something serious, like what I wanted to tell Dad about, and then burst out laughing. Or they'll get as angry as a nest of bullants when you do the slightest thing wrong which wasn't really wrong anyway, just that you did it at the wrong time or place.

That happened one day when I was cleaning out Bluey's cage. Every week, when I remembered, I put clean newspaper in his cage, taking the old piece outside, with its scraps of seeds and other things, and throw it on to the compost heap to turn into soil. I'd put fresh water in, and new seeds, and give the bell a polish if it was Christmas or his birthday. (He had birthdays once a month, and another one when I won a race in the school sports, which was fairly often.)

While I was doing all that, of course, I had to let Bluey out of the cage, so he usually had a good fly around the kitchen. The flies used to fly around the kitchen, too, but as Bluey was a budgie and not a flycatcher they weren't in any danger from him. They didn't realise that, though, so the kitchen was always a buzz of excitement on cleaning days.

The time when it happened was in the middle of our hottest summer, three days before the pigs got loose, so it was an interesting week. All the blinds were down and all the curtains were drawn. All the inside doors were open and all the outside doors were closed. You could have made a cup of tea with Blue's water, and his birdseed was starting to toast. It was the perfect day to clean him out.

The main trouble was the open doors. A bit of extra trouble was that it was surgery time. And the biggest trouble of all was that Mrs Phelpps was in seeing the doctor about something and Bluey flew into Mrs Phelpps's hair and did something in it that couldn't just be taken outside and thrown on the compost heap to turn into soil, and the doctor was my father.

He jumped up and tried to catch Bluey but only caught what Bluey did in Mrs Phelpps's hair, and quite a bit of her hair as well, and Mrs Phelpps did a bit of jumping, too, and Dad didn't like that a bit at all, and then they both fell over onto Dad's weighing machine, Dad under the Maid of the Mountains, and the scales grinding into Dad's back and then smashing into pieces under the strain.

By the time they'd got themselves untangled Bluey was back in his cage and I was in my room doing some homework for once, but none of that helped very much.

Because of all this experience I knew that I'd have to be very careful about when I told Dad. He seemed to be in a pretty good mood today. He'd washed and polished the car after its trip to the Show, and Bill hadn't been hurt too much when he fell off the bull and landed in the fairy floss machine, on his stomach with his mouth open. Mum had been cooking all day, almost, and the afternoon smells had been Dad's favourite meal getting itself ready, and Miss Hendley had finally allowed Bill to start writing with a pen instead of a pencil. This had been worrying Dad for some time because he thought that people should be able to write properly, or at least other people. He didn't count, as everybody knew that doctors had special fingers that stopped them from writing words that other people could understand, unless they were Arabs or Sandskrits.

Maybe dinner time tonight would be the right time, or straight afterwards. I'd have to make sure that everything went right for him, which would probably be a little difficult with Bill around.

'Dinners ready! Wash hands, everybody.'

The call to arms, and even old Brissy staggered out of the cool passage into the dining room. I gave my hands an extra-good wash, flannelled my face till it was rosy, and even almost decided to brush my teeth so my breath'd be fresh, but it would have taken too long working out which of the five tubes of toothpaste I should use.

Dad was already sitting at our big round table, with a bottle of wine opened beside him. That was a good sign, but they never opened one when Miss Hendley gave *me* a pen.

'Hello, Possum,' he said. 'Have a good day?'

I thought that I was going to be all right.

'Bill. Come on. Dinner's ready,' Mum called.

'Coming,' said the front-end loader.

'Yes, thanks, Dad. What about you?'

I didn't usually ask those sorts of questions because I wasn't all that interested in what Dad did; it was what *I* did that was important, but tonight was different.

'Terrific. We didn't have a rush at all today. Mrs Owen came in for a mixture to get her son going. Mr Gibson wanted some injections before he goes overseas next month. And Mrs Phelpps didn't come in again!'

I thought that his back was still a bit sore, and his front, so I changed the subject.

'Reanney said we were going to have a phantom-mine next month.'

'Oh. I think he meant 'pantomime'. I wonder if they'll ask me to be the MC again?'

'They might, Dad. They really liked your jokes last year.' I tried to say *really* but I couldn't: Dad's jokes are terribly weak. In fact, if they got any weaker they'd be like a fortnight, but he didn't know that and tonight wasn't the time to tell him.

'Bill. I'm putting the dinner out,' Mum called, a little louder than last time.

'Coming,' said Mr Punctuality.

Mum never did actually put the dinner out, only the dog; she always brought the dinner in.

'I've got a few new jokes to tell you tonight,' said Dad, already starting to smile. 'And a story.'

I wasn't quite so sure that I was going to be all right after all.

'That's good, Dad. I can't wait.'

'I'll tell you one straight away then,' he leapt.

'No no, Dad,' I leapt back. 'We'd better wait till the others come in.'

'Of course. They wouldn't want to miss out.'

Miss Out was a young lady I wished I didn't have to meet but I had to go through with it. There was no escape. I just hoped it was all going to be worth it in the end.

'Bill! Dinner's on the table!!' said Mum, quite a bit louder than before. As you can see she even put in two exclamation marks, which was probably to make up for the fact that she wasn't telling the truth.

'How many injections does Mr Gibson have to have?' Dad loved me asking doctor questions.

'Three. Cholera, typhoid, and small pox.'

That meant three lots of money for us. Why didn't other people go overseas too?

'Where does he have to have them, Dad?'

As soon as I'd said that I realised I'd made a mistake. I'd meant to ask when he had to have them, which was much safer. Now I was in for more embarrassment.

Dad saw me going pink, so he put in the reddening bit.

'In his er um....arm.'

'Bill! Come now. Your dinner's getting cold,' cried Mum, from just behind my ear, forgetting a couple of exclamation marks.

It wasn't even on the table yet, but we knew what she meant.

'Just a minute. I'm just finishing something.'

He was the same at bath time. It took half the night getting him in and the rest of the night getting him out. And even then he hadn't washed himself.

Mum put a great pile of roast chicken in front of Dad, and a plateful less for me. It was easy to see where Bill got his appetite from.

'I'm not calling you again. Come now!'

'In a minute.'

A minute was supposed to be a minute part of an hour, but with Bill they meant about the same thing.

Roast potatoes came next, and roast pumpkin, the potatoes around the outside and the pumpkin in the middle, like Red Indians attacking a wagon train crossing the prairies.

'You're going to miss out on dinner if you don't come straight away.'

'I've nearly finished. I've just got to do a bit more.'

Mum brought in a dish of peas from our garden, and a bowl of cauliflower and white sauce. The table was starting to fill up quite nicely.

'I'll give your dinner to Brissy if you don't come this instant.'

'Coming,' said Bill, which is what he said two pages ago, so you know that he'd nearly run out of things to say.

'When you were little you thought that the settlers crossed the fairies,' laughed Dad.

He'd got it all wrong again. It was the Indians I always got mixed up with. I couldn't work out how they got red, or why they lived in America instead of India.

A jug of steaming gravy wafted under my nose and I knew that I'd have to have some with a piece of bread later, if I had any room left.

'William! I'm going to sit down now and if you're not here when I do you'd better watch out'

'I'm packing the things away,' said Bill, proving that he hadn't quite run out of things to say.

Mum put the salt and pepper on the table and sat down as Dad poured her a glass of wine, a lovely clear yellow colour that tasted awful.

'Where's my dinner?!' yelled Bill, cross at being kept waiting, and a little worried that Mum might actually have given it to Brissy.

'It's in the oven. Be careful when you get it out – the plate's hot.'

Brissy hadn't got Bill's dinner once in all the years that she was told she was going to get it. She didn't even bother to look up nowadays, or dribble.

'Did you hear how the famous bike rider escaped from the Antarctic when his plane crashed?' burst Dad. He couldn't wait.

'Dad's going to tell us some new jokes,' I explained to the others. 'And a story,' I added, trying hard to sound interested.

'Boy!' said Bill. 'Tell us the rest of the story you didn't finish when the koala scared you!'

'Koala? Oh, yes. I do have a story about a koala. Now, how does it go?'

He was hopeless telling stories. Or jokes. He'd forgotten about the bike rider at the South Pole.

'What about the bike rider, Dad?' I asked, to help him back on the road.

'The bike rider? Oh, the bike rider! Yes. How did the bike rider escape from Antarctica?'

'When his plane crashed.'

'Yes, when his plane crashed.'

The potatoes were starting to get cold.

'Well, how did he escape?' Might as well get it over with, so we could start eating.

'He road away on his icicle!!'

Thank goodness that was over.

Dad beamed at everybody, putting a bit of light on our faces that we hadn't quite managed to get there on our own.

We helped ourselves to the vegetables and poured the delicious gravy over the lot, except the cauliflower.

'Did you know why almonds and armies are the same thing?' spurted the comic king from the other side of the table. It wasn't all over.

'Almonds and armies are the same because they're both full of colonels!' said Dad, almost falling off his chair.

'You don't have kernels in armies,' said Bill. 'They're nuts.'

I didn't say anything.

'You like words, don't you, Liss?' asked Dad. It looked as though he was moving off his jokes, but you couldn't be sure.

'Have you noticed that if you take the 'i' out of 'said' you get 'sad'? You'd get sad, too, if you lost your only eye!!'

I could see that he wasn't really leaving his jokes behind: he was just making them harder to understand.

'Can I have some more potatoes, please Mum,' said Bill. I didn't put a question mark in there because he didn't, and no one expected him to. It was surprising that he'd waited so long to finish his firsts and start on his seconds, thirds, and fourths.

'Here's another one,' said Dad, his food hardly touched yet, which Bill had already noticed. 'Why do you think your mother is called a 'woman'?'

I hadn't ever really given that idea much thought up until now. I usually thought of her as 'mum' or 'mother' or, when I saw some of the people in town, as a lady.

'Well, first you have 'man,' then you add some 'woe'!' he shouted, knocking over his third glass of wine.

Mum threw a terrible look at him that was supposed to look terrible, but Dad didn't seem too frightened, even though he cowered in his chair, whimpering, and waving his serviette in surrender as the wine dripped on to his lap.

'Woe to man equals woman!' he laughed again. 'Or without a man it's just woe!'

He kept on adding an 'e' to the 'wo,' which was just like a man — they always thought it was the little bit extra that counted, but *we* knew when enough was enough.

'What about the story, Dad?' said Bill as he finished off the last of the pumpkin.

Dad wiped the tears from his eyes, poured himself a new glass of wine, and began to eat his chicken.

'The story? You all think that I can't tell stories.'

That was true, at least up until our holiday with Granddad.

'No we don't, Dad. Go on, tell us another one, all spooky and dripping with blood.'

'Not such a scary one as last time, Dad. Bill got really frightened.'

'I did not! I don't get scared of anything!'

'Oh, yair! Why'd you have to change your pants then!?'

'I did not! I was just...sweating a lot in front of the fire.'

'This one's about a koala. It's a rather strange tale.'

'It would be if it was about a koala,' crowed Bill. 'They haven't got a tail!'

The goose bumps started up my legs again, a flock on each side.

'Many years ago there was a koala. He was only a young fellow, but he was big and bold. Soon he became bored with life in the tall manna gum trees, one bough being much like any other bough, even to an actor like him. Every time he climbed out on a limb he yearned to branch out himself, to see new places, to have adventures.'

'Sounds like Blinky Bill,' muttered our blinking Bill.

'One day he decided that he must do it. As he sat in a fork in the tallest tree in the forest he realised that he had come to a fork in his life, that he'd received a trunk call to the future

'Quickly he packed his bag – spare shoes, long trousers, a thick woollen jumper, fleecy-lined shirt, a dark brown overcoat, and three pairs of socks.

'He put on his best walking shoes, a pair of tough leather shorts, a rain-proofed jacket, and a knitted cap. Then he shinned and kneed down the tree to the crinkly forest floor and looked around. Should he go up hill or down hill? He knew that to go down hill was not the best thing to do when you're starting an adventure, and he knew that going up hill was hard work, even if you're young and bold. So he went across the hill, keeping to the contours and curves of the land.'

'Any sweets, Mum?'

'Gradually the land sloped down to the dry and dusty plains, away from koala country. He was leaving the trees, leaving the leaves. He turned and bowed to the boughs that were his home for so long, to the trunks without elephants, to all that he knew, to where he'd grown up to be as old as he was now

'He sighed, and turned his back, away from the past, into the future.'

The jokes were still coming, weren't they.

'His best walking shoes squeaked (he should've paid for them) as he set off across the plain. He wished he could fly, but it wasn't that sort of plain. Slowly the hills, his hills, receded into the distance, and the future became the present, burning fiercely on his knitted cap so that the sweat and even the perspiration poured down over his furry eyebrows.

'The sun beat on his capped head, making him dizzy. His eyes started to swim, even though he hadn't dived in anywhere. Shapes began to shimmer in front of him, calling him on, to shade and shelter and a cool sherbet.

'But when he arrived there was nothing there, only more heat. "What can I do?" he cried, his tongue nearly as furry as his little tail.'

I wished *Dad*'s tale was little.

"'I must take off my knitted cap!" he cried. And he did. On he went, bravely, even doggedly, except that he was a koala. "Oh, this heat!" he cried. "Where are my trees?" But there were no trees.

"'I must take off my rain-proofed jacket!" Even out here on the parched plain he could still think clearly. It wasn't going to rain before he got there, he could see that.

'On he staggered, through dried-up watercourses, over sand dunes. He was entering the Great Desiccated Desert, feared by all and survived by none, but he wasn't to know that. Even if he had he would still have pressed on. On.

"'I must take off my best walking shoes!" he cried. Off they came, laces and all, and he padded on through the sand, heroically, grittily on the gritty ground.'

I'd almost forgotten what I wanted to tell Dad. When was this story going to end??

'It was getting hotter and hotter! "I must take off my tough leather shorts!" he cried, and he struggled out of them, stumbling and almost falling with exhaustion. He could hardly walk. His feet were blistered. His tongue was swollen. His eyelids were closed. His breath was coming in short pants (almost the only clothes he still had on), but he couldn't stop. He couldn't take off any more clothes. It wouldn't be *right* to take off any more clothes.

'After all, how much could a koala bare!!?'

'Are there any more sweets, Mum?' said Bill.

Dad looked at us, waiting for us to laugh, but we couldn't. We'd waited so long for the end that when it came we weren't ready for it. Our laughing muscles had gone to sleep. And, in any case, it was one of the oldest jokes in the book. Even Mr Braden had heard it.

Dad looked so shocked that I thought that he might need to see a doctor, but as he was the only one around he'd have to go into the bathroom, and look in the mirror.

Mum and Bill began clearing away the things and I suddenly remembered what I had to tell Dad.

'Dad.'

'Yes, dear,' he replied, coming out of shock.

'Dad, can I tell you something?'

'Of course you can.'

'You won't laugh?'

'No, I won't laugh. It doesn't seem to be a laughing night tonight.'

'Well, you know Jemmy?'

'From Quimbilong? Yes, I know him.'

'And you know how he saved me at the Show, when Emperor Gum IV was carrying me off to get killed?'

'Yes, I remember that very well. It was only last week.'

'You promise you won't laugh?'

'I promise!'

'I'm going to make him my boy friend now, instead of Jingo. Stop laughing!! You promised you wouldn't laugh!! You SAID!!!!`

You can't trust anyone these days.

7

Bush Dance

...where everything doesn't quite work out.

I looked amazing. I was the biggest surprise in our mirror's life. And in mine.

Mirrors were usually a bit of a problem for me because they never showed me as pretty as I really was. Somehow or other they seemed to make my nose a little longer than it really was, my eyes a slightly different colour, and some of my expressions not as nice as I was really making them.

In my room I'd practise for hours writing my autograph in all sorts of ways, for when I was a famous actress or model, then I'd go into the bathroom and try out dramatic poses and expressions. The trouble was that the mirror didn't make them as good as they were inside my head. Whenever I looked at myself I kept catching my eye, and stared at myself until I got sick of it and had to drag my eyes away from my eyes. That was when I did my best expressions, the Oscar-winning ones, but as I couldn't see them I never knew what I looked like.

Getting ready to sign autographs was all right, but getting ready to be a famous actress was a bit difficult.

That afternoon Mum had torn up one of Dad's old shirts into strips, to make them ready for getting me ready that night. She didn't ask Dad about that, which was something I'd noticed before. Quite often I'd see Dad stumping around the house, looking for a coat or a jumper or a shirt, and never finding it until he'd forgotten what he was looking for. That was just as well, because Mum had usually thrown it out or made something else out of it, or given it away to the poor people in America or somewhere. Before dinner that night I had to get out of my dress and sit on the stool in the bathroom, with a towel around my neck, hoping that Bill wouldn't come in and see me. Then Mum washed my hair in the basin, with lots of lovely hot water and her best soap, followed by lots of not-so-nice cold water to get rid of the soapsuds (but not the smell) and to stop me catching cold, and then she rubbed my head so hard that I started to think of Red Indians again. When she'd finished my head was tingling all over and my hair was tangling all over

That meant that the worst part was on its way –
combing it out.

You've probably read in the newspapers about the
horrible torturing that bad people do in lots of other
countries, and I hate the sound of it, but you never read
about what mothers do to their innocent little daughters
every time they're going to go out somewhere.

The comb is a weapon as dangerous as a stock whip,
except that you can probably get away from a whip. Have
you ever tried getting away from your mother when she's
attacking you with a comb?!

It was easy to see why Red Indian mothers were called
squaws – they made their children squawk, which was the
same as in our bathroom as Mum dragged the comb
through my half-wet hair, like Dad raking up the lawn
after rain. First one side, then the other, then the back.
Over knots like a stump-jump plough. Through the
streaks of hairs like an explorer hacking a trail through the
jungle. Each movement pulling out at least a hundred of
my beautiful tresses. One day I'd have to buy a wig.

How is it that a comb can go through all that, handing
out so much pain, without losing its teeth? I nearly

ground mine to pieces just feeling it wrench through my hair.

When the combing was all over and Mum'd stopped shouting at me she gave me a good brushing. I liked that very much (except when I'd been yelling too much and Mum brushed my bottom a few times). It almost made me go to sleep. The tingling turned into a nice warm glow and I knew that my brain underneath was feeling pretty good, too. It's not often that you can do something good for your brain.

Last of all came the strips, which Mum had to do before Dad discovered that his shirt was missing. It sounds a bit strange saying that – how can you discover something when it's missing? Anyway, I think that Dad was out on a call so we got on with it without any interruption

First Mum ran her fingers through my hair, making a small ponytail. Then she wound one of the strips around it, from top to bottom, tying it at both ends. She did the same with a bunch of hairs next to the first one, and so on, right around my head, except for the front. I must've had a dozen striped ponytails by the time she'd finished, made from one of Dad's Pacific island shirts. "Pacific" means peaceful, but that was the wrong word for what I looked like.

I looked amazing.

There was one small problem that was bothering me a little, and which might have needed sorting out before the dance. I'd more or less told Jemmy about the new situation, about him being my boy friend now, but I hadn't seen Jingo since the show, so he wouldn't know. I wasn't all that sure that Jemmy knew, either, because when I told him he pretended to run away and hide. He was a faster runner than I was, but I was a faster thinker and, anyway, I knew that he wanted to get caught. I let him disappear behind the boys' shelter shed whilst I scampered quietly around the girls' shed. We met under the peppercorn tree and I gave him a quick cuddle before the bell went and he raced off....he didn't speak to me again that day – it was our secret.

The trouble was that both Jemmy and Jingo would turn up at my place to take me to the dance, and if they arrived at the same time I'd get terribly embarrassed and Dad would start laughing again. And goodness knows what Bill would do.

The bush dance happened nearly every year in Niamong, right in the middle of winter, when we had mud instead of dust, and thunder and lightning covered the sky. Everyone came to the bush dance, whether they could dance or not – it didn't seem to matter. Even the kids were allowed to go, the younger ones in pyjamas and dressing gowns, and slippers for a while, and the older ones dressed up properly.

This was my first year going dressed up, and I was going to look terrific. I loved dancing and I loved dressing up, so when the two came together on the same night I knew that the R.S.L. hall would be a little like heaven. Did you notice that word then? Together. To-gether. It seemed to be just the right word for what all the boys would want to be doing at the dance, when they saw me.

Dinner was quite a trial that night.

'What's your head bandaged for, Liss?'

'Hair today and gone tomorrow, Liss.'

'Comb into the garden, Maude, Liss.'

'Who's given you the brush off, Liss?'

It went on like that all through the meal. I could see that awful jokes passed down through the male side of the family, from father to son. Why they were called sons I'll never know, because they certainly weren't very bright.

Luckily Dad didn't seem in the mood to tell any of *his* dreadful jokes – he just kept staring at the strips in my hair, with a puzzled look on his face, those funny lines stretching up from his eyebrows up across his forehead and disappearing into the top of his head.

At last it was time for bed and peace. Although I was sure that I wouldn't go to sleep. Mum read me a story and then Dad gave me a tickled back and then they turned out the light and then I heard a rooster crowing.

I decided to get up straight away and have breakfast before Bill woke up.

After breakfast Mum and I walked down to the hall to help put up the decorations. We left Bill at home, trying to do some homework about our house. He kept on making mistakes and rubbing them out and bending the paper and wetting the paper with his tears. I almost felt sorry for him, because he was trying so hard to do good work for once. Why do you always make mistakes when you're trying to do your best work? When it doesn't matter about mistakes, you don't make them.

Mr Rawlinnson had cut a lot of branches off some gums and brought them in in his ute. Mr Brister had brought in about twenty bales of straw and Mr Grainger, the younger one, was scattering buckets of sawdust on the floor, to make it good for dancing on. I think he must've brought the sawdust straight from his butcher's shop, because I could see bits of fat and blood mixed up in it. He'd put half a dozen spare buckets out in the kitchen for later, just in case they were needed, and some blowflies were already busy around them, looking for suitable homes for their children.

Inside the hall were piles of ladies and kids, some up ladders and others standing on chairs, hanging streamers and balloons. Up on the stage Mr Manderson was getting his drums ready. He saw me and gave me a crinkle-faced smile, and his big bass drum a bit of a kick in the side to warn it that it had to do some work tonight.

We stayed there helping till about three o'clock, then Mum decided that it was time to go home and have a rest, as we'd be up very late that night. Everything was looking pretty good, even though it wasn't finished, and I couldn't wait to get back after dinner. I'd been wearing one of Mum's old scarves while we were doing the decorations because I hadn't wanted anyone to see my hair in the strips of Dad' old shirt.

When we got home Mum made up a light meal for us all and then we began the final getting ready time. This was the moment I'd been waiting for, when the strips came off. Mum carefully undid the knots, only breaking two of her fingernails along the way, and there I was, with twelve beautiful ringlets, each one curling around a tunnel of nothing. I reminded myself of the fairy tale about the ugly duckling that turned into a swan, except that I was far more beautiful.

Mum'd made me a new white dress, with pink flowers dotted on it, and a lace belt which did up at the back in a big bow. Jemmy would be proud of me. So would Jingo, but he'd probably also be a bit jealous because I wasn't his any more.

In between looking for his old tropical shirt Dad had spent a couple of hours washing and polishing the car so that its black paintwork gleamed, reflecting the sunset and me as I stepped gracefully down the steps, holding out my lovely dress carefully, pausing at the car door to make sure it was still shiny, and then settling myself on the back seat so that the dress wouldn't be crushed. Bill burst through the other door and crushed the dress, so I did what the Queen would have done and punched him on the nose, before Mum and Dad arrived.

I couldn't see Jemmy coming up the drive for me, or Jingo, either. They'd be quite upset that they'd missed me, but parents don't understand about these things so I hadn't mentioned that they'd be coming for me. I'd make it up to the boys later. Jemmy could have more than his fair share of dances with me. So could Jingo, for old times' sake

There was a traffic jam outside the R.S.L. hall. Cars and utes were pulling up in front of the door, their lights shining in the dark, lighting the ladies in their best dresses and frocks and the children in their nightclothes or whatever.

Dad stopped by the door and everyone turned to look at me as I climbed out.

Jemmy lived out at Quimbilong, which was quite a way away, so I wasn't all that surprised that he hadn't come before we left, but Jingo could've come. He only lived down in the main street and, after all, he didn't know that it would've been a waste of time.

Still, they'd be along later, and I'd have to choose which one to dance with first. It would probably be Jemmy, but if he still hadn't arrived by then I'd let Jingo have a go.

They'd both arrived! They were both inside, laughing and strutting around like bantam roosters waiting for their hens to lay an egg.

I held Mum's hand and didn't look at them, much. I ignored them, I turned my head away from them, I didn't listen to their merry laughter, I didn't even think about them and I'd never talk to them again, either of them, bull or no bull, Jingo or Jemmy.

'Hiya, Liss. You look terrific!'

'Thank you, Jemmy, yes I do, don't I.'

'You're the best looking girl here, Liss.'

'Thank you, Jingo, yes I am, aren't I.'

They were really very nice boys. I shouldn't have been so hard on them. I decided that I'd probably dance with each of them all night, till the moon went down and the musicians collapsed from exhaustion, and everyone went home, tired and happy, knowing that they'd watched the best dancing ever seen in Niamong.

'See ya later, Liss.'

They walked away up the hall, up near the men's end. I don't mean where the toilets were, but where all the men were standing around, talking about the sheep and the mud.

Mum and I took our cold chicken and pikelets out to the kitchen, where most of the women and a few of the ladies were bustling around. Mounds of food were stacked up all over the benches, mostly chicken and pikelets, but some turkey and drop scones, with splashes of green and orange showing where the rabbit food was. The giant urn was steaming in the corner, ready for making the cups of tea at the end of the dance. In the other corner, next to the stove, were the buckets of sawdust Mr Grainger'd brought in that morning, to keep the dance floor smooth. The blowflies were still there because of the nice warm stove, and if you're a fly you're blowed if you're going to turn up the chance of a feed, even in the middle of winter, at night.

I could smell sausage rolls heating up in the oven, which was another reason for the flies to be awake. "Heating" is only eating with an aitch, so I was pretty sure that the flies would be out of luck at suppertime. They'd have been better off staying with the bits of fat and blood in the sawdust.

Back out in the hall Mum and I walked over to the ladies' end, which was opposite the men's end, and both of them were at the sides, anyway. Old wooden chairs sat along the walls, waiting to do what they were made for, but not looking all that excited about it. The lights under their brown shades splashed pools of light onto the floor, making patterns where they couldn't do their job properly because of the streamers and bunting. Gum branches leaned against the walls, leafing quietly through their memories, and the bales of straw were obviously quite pleased that they weren't going to be eaten yet, even though they were tied up for the night and ran the risk of being sat on by at least one of the McPhees.

The hall looked wonderful, and smelled even better.

All of Mum's friends were there, and just about everybody who wasn't exactly her friend but who knew her, anyway. They all wanted to talk to her, now that she wasn't with Dad, and Mum wanted to talk to them. She loved talking and they loved talking. From what I could see most of them talked a lot without thinking too much. They just chatted, mostly, though I noticed that some of them backchatted and quite often I thought that hardly anyone was listening to what anyone else was saying. I had a lot to learn about talking to grown-ups, or rather about how grown-ups talked to each other, although talking to them wasn't really difficult – it was getting them to answer that was the problem.

The hall was humming by now, even though the McPhees weren't there. Up on the stage Mr Manderson came through the forest to check his drums again and wave to all his friends on the floor. He sat down and flicked the drumsticks expertly over the snaredrums and crashed them on to the cymbals, kicking the bass drum all the time. Everybody stopped to listen, the men tapping their feet on the floor and the boys pounding their arms up and down and kicking the straw bales hard enough for them to think that being eaten mightn't be so bad after all.

With a final blur of speed Mr Manderson weaved his sticks across all the drums at once, thumping the bass drum till it bounced on the boards, and spinning the cymbals in a frenzy, making our ears buzz like a swarm of locusts, and then he held his arms straight above his head, sticks spearing triumphantly towards the roof, and we stamped and cheered.

Slowly he lowered his arms and came towards the edge of the stage, most of his face hidden by laughing lines.

'Thank you, ladies and gentlemen, boys and girls. Welcome to this year's Bush Dance! I hope all you pretty girls have got on your best dancing shoes?'

Everybody looked at me when he mentioned pretty girls.

'What about all you handsome boys? Have you picked out your dancing partners yet?'

I looked at Jemmy, but he'd moved behind his father. Jingo was behind Jemmy.

'Doesn't the hall look terrific! What a great job every body did today! And what about the food out there! Why don't we forget the dancing and start the eating!'

I saw Bill start to move towards the kitchen and Dad pull him back. He didn't know Mr Manderson was joking. In fact he didn't realise that you *could* joke about food, unless you'd eaten it all already.

'Enough of this nonsense!' said Mr Manderson. 'I'd like now to introduce to you the rest of the band!'

There wasn't room on the stage for the rest of the band, only about two of them, which was why the rest of them weren't there. There weren't any others, anyway, so

I didn't know what he was talking about. We'd be lucky if they'd been able to find a pianist after last year.

'On the keyboards!...that's the piano for all you out there who aren't familiar with musicians' talk – on the keyboards we have....!'

He paused to make sure that we were all listening. We all were, except for little Timothy Phillips, who'd gone to sleep on a bale of straw.

'On the keyboards we have.....*Miss Hendley*!!!'

Scratcher started to cheer a split second before everybody else, and then split behind two grown-ups as everybody laughed at him and cheered Miss Hendley. She came on in a fairly nice dress and gave quite a nice curtsy, mainly towards the men's side, and sat at the piano. You've probably noticed already that if you drop off the aitch and forget about the why in Miss Hendley's name you almost end up with Pendle, which just goes to show that you don't need a lot of· letters after your name, or even in front of it, to be someone special. I won't say what you have to do to finish turning Hendley into Pendle, because it's a bit rude.

Everybody started to move away from the walls, getting ready for the first dance, which was usually a trot of some sort. I still hadn't made up my mind about Jingo or Jemmy. It really should be Jingo to have the first dance with me, as a sort of goodbye present, but then, on the other hand, Jemmy was probably thinking that he should have the first one because it was going to be the first time that we'd be together like that, after the bull.

'Wait a moment you impatient people! There's more to come!'

Mr Manderson was shouting above the hubbub, which was mainly on top of our heads. We all stopped talking and milling, and looked up at him.

'I said I was going to introduce the band to you! A piano and drums isn't a band!'

We all knew that, but it was all we'd ever had.

'For a band to be a band you need....a....saxophone!!'

Everyone cheered again, but with puzzled looks coming out of their mouths. No one in Niamong played the saxophone. Someone's friend must've come up from Melbourne or somewhere. Or it was April 1st. We all looked as Mr Manderson marched back to his drums and gave a long roll on them.

'Ladies and gentlemen! Boys and girls! It is with the very greatest pleasure that I present to you, for the first time on any stage, especially this one, Niamong's own, Niamong's one and only, Niamong's saxophonist supreme!......'

We all pressed to the front of the hall, the boys jumping up and down at the edge of the stage.

'...Mrs Phelpps!!'

There were three loud crashes.

The first as the boys panicked out the door.

The second when the rest of us fell forwards onto the front of the stage, into the space where the boys had been.

And the third when Mrs Phelpps came on, tripping on the hem of her dress, sending her saxophone flying, like a mirrored comet, into Mr Manderson's drums, which then marched, rolled, and flying-saucered into what Mr Grainger had put on the floor that morning.

I thought that was the best beginning to a bush dance we'd ever had, and as we all started to get up from the floor it seemed that everyone agreed with me. They were all talking to each other and laughing and pointing and helping put the drums back on the stage, and three or four of the bigger and stronger men helped Mrs Phelpps to stand up, whilst Miss Hendley brushed down Mrs

Phelpps's dress and propped up her music stand, and the boys crept back in.

Gradually the band sorted itself out and Miss Hendley played a few notes on the piano to make sure that all the black ones hadn't gone up to one end. Mr Manderson rearranged his drums and grinned at us a bit more carefully this time, and Mrs Phelpps hefted the saxophone around her neck, twitching her fat fingers over the levers.

'The first dance will be a foxtrot,' announced Mr Manderson, the first man I'd ever heard talking when Mrs Phelpps was around, except for Mr Braden, of course.

I think he was only able to make his announcement because Mrs Phelpps had half the saxophone in her mouth, getting ready to trot the fox around the paddock.

He counted one two three four, tapping his feet on the floor, Miss Hendley played the introductory bars, and then Mrs Phelpps blasted as though she was blowing up the Sydney Harbour Bridge single-handed. Or I should say, double-lunged. I know that last half word looks like lunged, but it's really lunged, but in any case they were both the right word as far as Mrs Phelpps's playing was concerned.

The men stood up and started to come towards us, husbands going for their wives (which was a change in many cases) and the older boys following behind, making for whichever girl they thought might be silly enough to have a dance with them.

I sat quietly, with my hands clasped properly on my lap, waiting for Jemmy to come over. I knew that he'd probably be a little while because the younger boys always had a bit of trouble pushing through the fathers and brothers.

I thought that I'd sit quietly waiting for Jingo, too, as he still didn't know about the new arrangements. We'd have a little chat for a few minutes, and then I'd tell Jingo that I was giving Jemmy the first dance, because he'd rescued me from the bull.

They seemed to be quite a while getting over to me; all the women and most of the ladies on our side had already been picked, so I had a quick look up to see what was keeping him, or them.

Dark-haired Meaghan and blond-haired Kate were walking across from our side to the boys' side! What were they doing!? They went straight up to Jingo and Jemmy and took them away and started dancing with them!

Didn't they know they weren't allowed to do that!?! Didn't they know that they had to let the boys ask them!? Didn't the boys know that they were supposed to ask me?!! I hated them. I wouldn't like them any more. Any of them. Especially Jingo and Jemmy. I foxed with Dad.

I didn't really dance with Dad – it was with his hips – but we managed to get around the floor a few times, and I could see that Jingo and Jemmy were a bit upset about missing out so I didn't mind too much.

The dying cat up on the stage finally died and Mrs Phelpps beamed puffily at us and we all clapped loudly so that the band wouldn't walk off in a huff and go home before we'd had enough. I thanked Dad for dancing with me and we all went back to our own sides of the hall while the band had a rest.

After a few minutes we felt the floor tremble and Mrs Phelpps came back on to the stage with the others.

Mr Manderson announced the next dance.

'Ladies and gentlemen! Girls and boys! Take your partners for the Pride of Erin!'

This time he counted one two three and all three of the band began together, almost.

The men and the older boys moved over towards us pretty well at the same time this time, the husbands going to their wives again and the boys looking for someone else.

I sat, twiddling my thumbs, waiting for one of the boys to come and ask me to dance, when suddenly I saw them ducking out to the toilet. I suppose that when you've got to go you've got to go, but why can't boys wait till the right time!

I erinned with Dad, as the rain began to fall on the iron roof, drumming along with Mr Manderson, but crying instead of smiling.

I forgot to thank Dad when we went back to our own sides, and I didn't bother to sit down because my dress was starting to get crushed.

The rain was coming down even more heavily when Mr Manderson called us to our feet again, this time for the barn dance. Everyone loved the barn dance because you got to dance with everyone for a minute or two. If you didn't like someone very much, or if they were a grown-up, you looked around the hall, working out how long it'd be before someone you did like came along. When he arrived you grabbed him before it was the right time and you didn't let him go until the next person along pulled him away from you.

But you could only go in the barn dance if someone asked you.

I stood against the wall, with my arms folded, searching for Jemmy or Jingo. They weren't there. They must've still been out in the toilet. How could they be so long? We hadn't even had anything to drink yet.

Dad took me out on to the floor. It wasn't too bad as I had a go with Ray and Ashley and Craig and Geoff and they swung me off my feet a bit. In fact I was starting to enjoy it when everyone went quiet, just as Mrs Phelpps was belting out a high note. It sounded like an air raid warning, which is what it was, really.

In the open doorway, the rain pouring down behind them, and off them and on to the dance floor, were the McPhees.

All of them. From Mr McPhee right through the whole pong of them to the youngest, his toes sticking out of a sandal and a gumboot, which had little bits of stuff sticking to it. The same stuff was sticking to the rest of them, too, in different places, so that the whole family seemed to be sticking together, like a farmyard.

The wind slammed the door shut, showing once again that nature is stronger than mankind, and that it'd rather have the McPhees inside with us than outside with it.

I think the lights dimmed a bit as the family moved across the hall towards the kitchen, and I saw a few eyes close as careless barn dancers got too close. The great circle of people that had stretched happily around the edges of the hall began to shrink towards the stage, where Mrs Phelpps's saxophone blowing gave them some safety.

Each of the McPhees carried a parcel or a basket or a box into the kitchen and put them up on the bench with the other food. I couldn't hear any grunting or squealing coming from them so they were probably full of ferrets.

When they came out again they paired off and started to do what they thought was the barn dance. It looked more like a snake trying to swallow a hippopotamus. Water and other things dripped off them, and steam and pong drifted into the air and clouded over the rest of us who were trying to mind our own business. In no time we had two circles – our big one, pressed against the wall and dancing with one foot on the chairs, and the McPhees' one in the middle, dead noses jerking around like anteaters that'd found bullants instead of termites.

Mr McPhee looked proudly at his family, which was nearly half of Niamong, and Mrs McPhee smiled her toothy smile at everyone. In fact she was so toothy that even her canines seemed to be barking. Dad said that the McPhees were the only family in the whole of the Niamong district who didn't have a wisdom tooth between them. Some of them didn't have all that many teeth, either.

The rain was crashing down now – we'd probably need an ark if it didn't stop before we went home. The outer circle was moving round the hall like a sleepy worm, bunch-bunching up over the chairs and stretching out across the doorways and the front of the stage. When I was nearly at the kitchen door I bumped into something, and then another something, both of them soft and both of them creeping. One of them looked like Jingo's jumper but they both disappeared into the kitchen before I could get a good look at them. By the time we'd inched our way up there the door was closed again.

If it was Jingo and Jemmy I bet they were after the food. It was a wonder Scratcher and Bill weren't with them. It'd serve them right if they opened the McPhees' things first.

I'd just about reached the other side of the hall when I heard a great yell coming from the kitchen, the door burst open, and Jingo and Jemmy pelted into the worm and the McPhees. Suddenly all the people near the kitchen door started to move a bit more quickly, even though the music was staying the same. I could see them all heading towards the McPhees, which you'd only normally do to escape a bushfire, so something must've been happening.

The men started yelling and the ladies and girls started shrieking and I saw lots of little shapes scurrying between their legs. THE MCPHEES HAD BROUGHT THEIR FERRETS!! It wasn't supper at all, which was probably just as well, anyway.

'Prince! Queenie! Duke! Duchess! Kingie! Earlie! Attila!'

McPhees were going everywhere. So were the ferrets because they'd got a whiff of the blood and fat in the sawdust on the floor. They scampered through the leaping legs, nipping whatever they thought was a morsel, whether it was dead or alive and still trying to dance. They ducked away from falling bodies and jumped over people scrabbling along the floor. They twisted and turned and snarled and bit.

The band played on till one of the largest ferrets stormed up the steps and disappeared under Mrs Phelpps's evening gown, which took up most of the stage and pretty quickly Mr Manderson as well. Miss Hendley jumped onto the top of the piano as the drums and cymbals fell off the stage again, closely followed by Mr Manderson, Mrs Phelpps, and the ferret, who couldn't have known what he'd let himself in for. Not that he knew much about anything ever again, as Mrs Phelpps was a very large thing to land on a ferret that hadn't been doing any bodybuilding courses.

Suddenly Graveyhead appeared in the middle of the floor with his old shotgun.

'Keep calm! Keep calm!' he yelled, and pulled the trigger. All the lights went out and the bunting and streamers poured down on top of us, mixed up with flying gum leaves and shafts of dirty straw.

'Keep calm! Keep calm!' yelled the same cracked voice out of the darkness. 'I've got a light!'

He had, too, and when he struck the match it promptly set fire to the streamers.

'Don't let the straw catch fire!' yelled someone. I think it was Dad, who was never really fond of barbecues.

The door slammed open and half a dozen men rushed out – I think they were the fire brigade. Then a bright light shone through the doorway: someone had driven a car round.

We started to sort ourselves out, standing up carefully. The lights went back on again and we blinked around at the disaster. Half the people looked like scarecrows and the other half looked like scared crows, ash on their faces from the burnt streamers. The floor looked like autumn in a butcher's shop. There were more red flowers on my dress than when we'd come, and they weren't exactly flowers.

And there were no McPhees.

And when we went into the kitchen to get our supper there was no supper either.

The ferrets had got there first.

8

Brissy

...where I have my saddest day.

How did it happen? How could it have
happened? She wasn't allowed to roam the
streets – she always stayed out the back or in
the house.

It couldn't have happened when we were
taking her for a walk, because we would have seen it
happen, even if it had been terribly embarrassing.

Brissy was going to have pups.

She was starting to get fat. Not the same way as Mum
did before she had Bill, but sort of *droopy* fat. Her tummy
seemed to fall down, with little knobs on it, but I wasn't
sure what they were. I thought they might've been the
new puppies' toes or something.

The thing was that we didn't have a father dog, and
without a father dog it's impossible to have a mother dog,
I think. Our house had a fence all the way around it,

nearly as high as me in the front, and higher everywhere else, so that any dogs who thought they might like to become father dogs would have an uphill battle – and we were keeping a sharp watch out.

We had heard a few noises, but that was probably possums, especially as it only happened at night. And sometimes we noticed a bit of mud on top of the fence, but that was probably Bill, so we really didn't know about the puppies until they were almost born.

It's no good having a father who's a doctor when your dog's having puppies – you need a vet. Vets do almost the same training at the university as doctors do, but doctors don't do almost the same as the vets. I could never imagine Dad asking Brissy to poke her tongue out. The only trouble was – we didn't really know that Brissy was having pups until it was almost too late. I think Mum and Dad were a little suspicious about the noises at night, and the mud on the fence, but because they never actually *saw* a father dog anywhere near Brissy they didn't worry, although they did talk about it sometimes. Then   one night, about the time when the nightmares are galloping through my head and around the room, I heard Dad leap out of bed and crash into their bedroom door, which he'd forgotten he'd closed so that the light wouldn't stop me going to sleep while they were reading. He yelled something and light fell into the passage and onto me. It didn't really hurt me, because it was quite light, but it certainly woke me up pretty quickly.

'What's happening, Dad?! Is the house burning down?'

'No! I heard a scrabbling under the house! I think it's Brissy!'

'Is she burying a bone or digging one up?'

'No! I think she's having pups!'

I thought *Dad* was having pups, the way he was carrying on.

'Why's she having them under the house? Why doesn't she go down to the hospital? Like Mum did.'

'*She* wasn't having pups!' said Dad, trying to get his left arm into the right sleeve of his dressing gown.

I thought that I'd better not say anything about that. He did up the cord at the back and rushed down the passage to the back door. He looked as though he was going in three directions at the same time, because he had his slippers on the wrong feet.

'Wait for me! I'm coming!'

In a second or two my dressing gown was on and my slippers were on, and my torch was on – because it was dark out there. I hurried down the passage to the back door, so that I wouldn't be too late, just in time to be knocked over as Dad came charging back in.

'My torch! My torch! I need a torch!'

Looking up at him from the floor I wondered if he was always like this when he was delivering babies. He probably sent the *fathers* into the room while he paced up and down outside.

'I've got a torch,' I said. 'It's a good bright one.'

'Come on, then!' he yelled, pulling the torch out of my hand and disappearing through the door.

I climbed off the floor and went out the back, following the light of the torch as it fell through the plumbago and strawberries.

By the time I'd reached the side of the house Dad had already climbed through the access door and was scuffling through the dust towards the front of the house, banging his head on the floor every few seconds.

(Under a house is the only place I know where you can bang your head on the floor when you move your head upwards, unless you're lying on your back, of course.)

'Hello, girl!' I heard Dad yell softly. 'How are you?'

Dust splashed into his face as her hairy tail whacked the earth, making him sneeze and bang his head again.

'There, there, girl. Are we having puppies?'

I *knew* we should've got the vet.

Brissy's great brown eyes looked at us, but she kept moving her head around, and sniffing. She didn't seem to know what was going on. She must've gone to the same medical school as Dad. She kept on getting up and twisting round and round, and lying down and getting up again.

'What's she doing, Dad?'

'I think she's trying to make a nest for her pups.'

'How can she make a nest without any feathers?!'

'They usually make a nest in the grass, a kind of snug place for the puppies to keep warm in.'

'Where are the puppies?' I thought they must be still inside her, because I could still see their toes sticking out.

'They're not ready to come out yet. She's just getting ready for them.'

'Why don't we bring her inside?'

'It's probably best not to disturb her. Come on, I think we'll go back to bed.'

We gave her a pat each, but she didn't seem to be interested. I don't even think she realised that pat was tap spelt backwards, either, but why should she when she was about to have a pup, which was the same backwards *and* forwards.

'You hop back into bed, Liss. I'll call you if anything happens.'

'All right, but I'll never go to sleep while Brissy's having pups.'

'Wake up!' shouted a voice crashing down the passage.

The sun was just coming up over the town, making the magpies sing about their breakfast and the crows tell us what Noah built in the bible. Frost covered the front lawn, the chooks out the back started to kerk, and the old rooster crowed a couple of times, which is what the crows should've done.

'One's out! One's out!' shouted the floor under my feet, so I raced out the back and around the side, even though it's pretty hard to imagine a round side.

'She's trying to bury it!' shrieked a voice between the stumps, and I heard Dad bang his head on the floor again.

The space under the floor looked like the Showgrounds the day I went for that ride on EG IV – dust was everywhere.

'Go and tell Mum that I'm bringing her into the laundry!'

I left him trying to find the pup that was buried and told Mum the good news about the laundry, but she'd heard it all through the floor.

Newspapers were everywhere. In the corner was an old suitcase, with the lid open and propped back against the wall. Inside the case she'd put some straw and bits of crumpledup paper. And she'd put the kettle on.

'Go and tell Dad it's all ready.'

Back under the house I went, with a handkerchief over my mouth and nose for the dust.

'What have you got that on for?' dusted Dad.

'You have to wear a mask when babies are being born. You should know that.'

'What did you bring the spade for?'

'To dig up the puppy she buried.'

Oh for a vet. Didn't he know anything about animals?!

'Is Mum ready yet? Why's she taking so long?'

'She was ready before you asked her.'

'Oh.'

I supposed P would come next. Little did I know.

Dad carried Brissy into the laundry and put her into the suitcase, and went back for the buried treasure.

Brissy didn't look terribly sure about what was going on, which was fair enough, I suppose, as it was her first set of babies. She kept turning around and looking between her back legs, and licking herself, and looking up at us.

'Look! Look! One's coming!'

Her tummy was moving around a bit, and then, suddenly, a long shining thing plopped out from between her legs. She looked at it, not knowing what to do.

'Lick it!'

Brissy looked at Dad and licked her lips.

'The puppy! Your baby! Lick it!'

'Lick it! Lick it!' shouted Dad quietly again. I thought Brissy had the right idea the first time. Who'd want to lick *that* slimy mess? Even to see what was inside.

She looked at the slightly wriggling thing at her back end.

She sniffed it.

And she started licking it.

'Good girl!' purred Dad. 'You're a very good girl! What a clever girl you are.'

I thought she was stupid. Slurp slurp slurp. It was revolting. And then she ate what shed licked off! She ate it!! Yurkk!!

And there was the most beautiful little animal you've ever seen in your life!

It was black, all over. Its eyes were shut tight, screwed up in its wonderful black face. Brissy licked it and licked it in great doggy kisses, telling it that she loved it, even though she didn't know it very well yet. It lay there, lapping it up, getting its strength to crawl over to have its breakfast. Then it mewed like a kitten and nuzzled into Brissy's tummy.

'How many puppies will she have, Dad?'

'I don't know, really. Perhaps seven or eight.'

Seven or eight!

'Here comes another one!'

Another flat wet balloon appeared. Brissy didn't waste much time getting off the slimy stuff so that it could have its breakfast, too. It was as black as the first one.

'They do look rather like Labradors, dear,' said Mum.

'Yes, they do. But we couldn't be that lucky could we?'

I didn't know what they were talking about, but I did see the next slug before they did. That made three black ones sucking at Brissy's tummy.

'Here's Number Four!'

'Number Five!'

'Number Six! Number Six is a white one!'

It was like the top of the milk – white but not quite white. And it was even more beautiful than the others, although I wouldn't have told them that. She looked just like Brissy.

It scrambled over to its mother and pushed its way into the middle of the others, so that there were two black ones on each side, and it started pulling away at Brissy's drinking fountains. The other four had bellies like balls and they'd more or less stopped drinking.

Number Seven was a white one, too.

'Seven,' said Dad. 'I think that'll be all.'

We sat at the kitchen table and watched our new family through the laundry door. Mum and Dad had a cup of tea, Dad rubbing his head a bit as he drank.

'What're we going to do with them, Dad?'

'I think they'll be all right in the laundry for a while,' said Dad.

'No, I meant when they get bigger.'

'Dad can make a run for them out the back. But we can't keep them, dear.'

'Why not? They're lovely!'

'Yes, but they grow up, and I'm not having eight dogs running around.'

'Nine. There's the one Brissy buried.'

'I'm afraid that one didn't make it, Liss. I think it must've been a little weak,' said Dad quietly. 'I didn't get to it in time.'

I was sad when he said that. Poor little thing. Then I noticed Brissy moving around in the suitcase.

'Dad! I think she's having some more!'

'She couldn't be!' said Dad, not quietly.

But she was. She had four more: two black ones and two white ones. How'd they all get a drink? I didn't think that she had enough taps.

'We might have to help her, with a bottle,' Dad said, even though I hadn't said anything out loud. But Brissy thought that that would be quite unnecessary.

The rest of that day I stayed in the laundry, watching the fluffy little things sleeping and drinking, and wriggling into a good spot for a drink, and then going to sleep with their little black noses snuffling against Brissy's tummy. Sometimes she'd get up and turn around and they'd all fall off and I'd have to put them back. They always woke up when they fell off, and discovered that they were hungry again so they had to start tugging at the milk supply again.

One day their eyes opened, all of them on the same day, even the littlest. By then there were nine pups left. I don't think she had enough milk for twelve, or she might have accidentally squashed them at night, but the nine left were really healthy and strong, waddling around just about on their fat tummies. Brissy seemed to be quite proud of them and I thought they looked lovely, the three white ones falling over the black ones, playing happily as they grew bigger.

We still had newspaper all over the floor, because they didn't know about the garden and what dogs are supposed to use the garden for, and Mum had to ask some of her friends for extra supplies. The bigger they grew the more layers of paper we had to put on the floor, and we had to keep on changing it.

I wanted to keep all the pups for ever, but after they were about ten weeks old Mum and Dad started finding good homes for them, and soon we were back to only

Brissy. I didn't think she minded all that much by then because I think she was getting a bit tired of being chased and bitten and sucked, but I missed them.

Mum and Dad talked about having a spade for Brissy so she wouldn't have any more pups and she went off to the vet for a couple of days. I didn't see why she couldn't have had our spade.

All that happened years before. Brissy never had any more pups, which just goes to show that spades are useful for other things besides digging up the garden. We did meet the father of the pups, though. He was a new dog who'd moved into Niamong not long before and who lived down near Jingo's place. And he was a Labrador! A black one, so that explained all the black pups and why they looked like Brissy, even though she was white.

I taught her to sit and lie, and to fetch a stick, and Bill taught her to bark when he came along. When I came home from school she'd be waiting for me at the gate, panting, and wagging her tail. We'd go for walks along the creek, and swim in the summer, her strong legs pulling her through the water nearly as quickly as I could swim. If I didn't watch out her long claws would scratch me, because when she was in the water she couldn't stop swimming, even when I was holding her.

And now she was old.

She'd stopped getting fatter a while ago, and started getting thinner. The whiskers along the sides of her mouth turned white, and after she met me at the gate we took a long time getting back up the hill to the house. The rabbits in the paddocks up the back became lazy and cheeky, hardly bothering to run away when we went for a walk up there, and she stayed pretty close to the track I was walking along.

Bill thought it was very funny when she fell over, or couldn't get up properly when she was lying down, and we all laughed a bit. Dad said she was getting arthritis, which made her joints stick.

One day Dad took her down to the vet. When he brought her home he said that the vet'd given her some tablets for the arthritis, to see if they would help. He said her heart was pretty good for a dog her age, even though it was a bit wonky. We crushed a tablet into her meal each night, and fussed over her to help her get better. She wagged her tail and licked us.

But she didn't get better and she didn't really eat her food. One day she couldn't stand up at all.

Mum and Dad were very quiet. I stroked her head and talked to her about her lovely puppies, and Bill tried to get her to drink some milk. She lapped up a few drops and licked a milky tongue over his fingers, and laid her head back tiredly on her rug.

'I think I'll take her back to Dr Hilton,' said Dad.

He picked her up gently, cradling her in his arms like a baby. Mum went off to her room.

'Give her a pat, son,' said Dad. 'Liss.'

We stroked the old girl down the passage.

'How long will she be down at the vet's, Dad?' asked Bill.

'I don't know. I'll see.'

He put her on the back seat of the car and drove slowly away down the hill.

9

Play Bill

...where I'm even more amazing than before.

For once Mr Braden was getting interesting. The blackboards were covered with sheets of butcher's paper, a little stained so I knew that they were from Mr Grainger's butcher's shop, and Mr Braden was standing at the front of the classroom, puffed up with importance like a tree that had more or less survived a bushfire.

Mr Braden didn't get interesting very often. Usually we called our room the class tomb, and everybody made those terrible grave jokes until we got sick to death of them and agreed to bury the whole subject till next time.

As we sat down we didn't say anything at all. We never said anything when we marched into the classroom anyway, because that'd mean a fair amount of trouble for us, but this time it was exactly different.

There was somebody else sitting at the back of the room, arms folded and an exercise book on his lap. He looked as though he'd started a few bushfires in his time.

'Good morning, girls and boys,' said Mr Braden, his face trying to smile but not quite remembering how to.

We were standing beside our desks, looking out the backs of our heads at the other man.

'Good morning, Mr Braden,' we said back to him.

'Say good morning to Mr Olney,' said Mr Braden.

We'd turned around before he'd closed his mouth.

'Good morning, Mr Olney,' we said, staring at him. I think I heard Scratcher call him Old Knee but I couldn't be sure.

'Mr Olney has come up from Melbourne to see you, children,' Mr Braden said.

We weren't listening, because we'd never seen a stomach as big as that before, even on Emperor Gum IV. The exercise book *had*n't been on his lap at all.

'Good morning, everyone,' mooed the man from Melbourne. 'I'm from the Education Department, and I've come to look at Your Work.'

When he started putting capitals onto his words I knew that we'd better be careful. No tricks today.

152

'You may sit down, now.'

That wasn't Mr Braden giving the orders for once, so we were pretty certain which end of the room our bread was buttered on.

'Thank you, Mr Olney,' said Mr Braden. 'Now, girls and boys, I have something rather special for you today.'

We thought that it was really Mr Olney that he had something special for, but that didn't matter, if it was special.

'Behind this paper,' said Mr Braden, waving a bush fly away, 'is something you've never seen before!'

Behind the paper were the blackboards, and we'd seen them before. Something else must be there, or on them, because I didn't think he'd dare to lie to us with Mr Olney up the back, watching him.

'This will be one of the most interesting things I've shown you, girls and boys,' said Mr Braden, brushing away a housefly that had just done something on the paper.

He sort of looked at Mr Olney when he said that, but not quite.

'I'll now take off the first piece of paper. Pay attention everybody,' said Mr Braden

Everybody was paying attention like anything, because two huge blowflies were doing something together on the butcher's paper that made me go pink. Mr Braden saw them and bellowed with rage, choking off in a strangled cough as he remembered who was sitting at the back of the room.

For a moment his hand didn't really care about Mr Olney from Melbourne and it crashed onto the butcher's paper, just missing the two flies and what might have turned into fifty other ones. The paper tore off in a great hurry and behind it we saw something that looked like this

Óloi oi ánthrōpoi gennioúntai eleútheroi

kai ísoi stēn axioprépeia kai ta dikaiṓmata.

'There! Do you see that!' said Mr Braden.

I heard the chair creak at the back of the room. I didn't know what Mr Olney made of the jumble on the board, but it was all Greek to me.

'It's Greek!' said Mr Braden, which just goes to show that you don't always need a teacher.

'Now look at this,' he said, tearing off the next sheet.

Underneath was another mess of lines. They looked Greek to me, too, but I didn't think that'd be right twice. For some reason they reminded me of dim sims.

'It's Ancient Egyptian!' he said, proving that it's wise not to jump to confusions. 'Isn't that interesting!'

By this time we were pretty sure what was underneath the next bit of paper, and all the other pieces, too. What time would the bell go?

'And now look at this one!'

How many languages are there?! Or ways of writing?

'And this one!'

We were getting sick of all those exclamation marks, but what can you do when you're Bradened at the front and Olneyed at the back?

The flies were having a terrible time trying to land on their lunch as Mr Braden whipped off the next and the next and the next bits of paper.

'Cyrillic! That's Russian. Named after St Cyril the Slav. And this one's Sanskrit!'

That was probably named after St Sand the Critter.

'Here's Arabic! And this one's Chinese!'

I knew we'd come to the dim sim sooner or later.

'What is it that's so interesting about all these?!!'

155

I certainly didn't know. *He* was supposed to be the teacher.

'They're all different from English!!' he shouted.

I *thought* there was something funny about them!

'And they're all the same! They always look the same!'

Even a mudlark could tell they were all different, and what was under the last piece of paper?

'They're always the same! Whenever you see some Arabic writing it's the same! When you see some Chinese writing it's the same! It's the same with Russian and Ancient Egyptian and Indian and Japanese and everything! Except English!!'

I thought it was time for the National Anthem.

'Only English is different! You can write the English alphabet in dozens of ways. Scores of ways. Even hundreds of ways! And You can Print it in scores of ways, too!'

I think he was right about writing. Everybody I knew wrote in a different way, especially Dad. I didn't know about all those other languages, but he was a teacher so he must've known what he was talking about.

'And now the last! Look at all these ways you can write the English alphabet!'

He ripped off the paper grandly, turning towards us as though he was a world-famous actor who'd just given the performance of his life.

All of that part of the board, where we were going to see the millions of different kinds of ways of writing English, was empty. Rubbed off.

Except, that is, for one sentence, written in bright light green, with a white and black border.

MR BRADEN CAN'T WRITE ENGLISH!

Mr Braden's border went white, then black.

Mr Olney's border was already black when we looked at him.

'WHO DID THAT!' they both shouted together, like a vice crushing our heads, and completely forgetting the question mark.

No one said anything, but when we all went through Mr Braden's office a few seconds later we found an extra pair of hands helping our bottoms out the door again.

****

Mr Braden wasn't the only actor in Niamong, although he was probably the only grown-up who tried to act every day. The town had decided to put on a revue in the RSL hall at the end of the year. That was what Reanney was talking about when he said we were going to have a phantomine or something. A revue is where everybody joins in and sings songs and does funny things, usually using old songs with new words about people who lived in the area, or about things that'd happened during the year.

This time I'd written a play.

Well, not exactly a play – they go on for hours and have people dying all over the place – it was really a sketch, but how you can call something a sketch when it's not a drawing I don't know.

The play was going to have Jingo in it, and Jemmy, and Robbie because he was bigger, and it was very funny, especially the end. And I had to tell everybody what to do in it, as well as write it.

The main thing that went wrong before the night was that they asked Dad to compere it again. Had they forgotten those jokes he told last year? Did they want him to try to make up another bunch of silly ones? And then laugh at them himself? Maybe they all liked seeing a doctor making a fool of himself and his daughter in front of everybody. I think it would be pretty good watching a doctor making a fool of himself, too – except when he's your father.

Dad was impossible all the time up to the revue. He'd walk around the house with his head in the clouds, mumbling and waving his arms in the air, and sniggering when he thought something was funny. Then he'd go into his study and write it down so he wouldn't forget it.

I just quietly wrote my play in my bedroom, without any fuss, except when Bill accidentally squished up the second page and sat on it.

Wooden chairs were set out in rows across the hall, so you couldn't see the burn marks on the floor. The piano and drums had been taken off the stage and put on the floor at the front. With a bit of luck Mrs Phelpps wouldn't be playing the saxophone.

Everybody who was putting on an act had to stay out the back when the people started coming in, so that the audience wouldn't get an idea of what was going to happen. The fire brigade had put up a great big tent out there, with trestle tables for putting things on, and camp stools for putting other things on, and several old mirrors for putting on the make-up. Jingo and Jemmy weren't all that keen on this bit, because they thought that somebody'd kiss them if they had make-up on, but I told them all actors had to wear make-up and if there was any kissing to be done I'd do it to any boys who didn't have any on.

Between the tent and the back door of the hall was a bit of a path and a few puddles, lit by a bare globe over the door. In charge of the door was Gravyhead, without his shotgun. He had a funny sort of scarf around his neck, and a pencil. His job was to tick off each act at the right time and let them through the door to the stage, or back out again after their act was over. He made it a bit harder for himself by locking the door each time with a big key which he had dangling from a string around his neck.

Suddenly there was a roll of the drums and a quivering of the piano. I heard lots of shuffling and coughing inside as they stood up for the National Anthem, and then more shuffling and coughing and talking as they sat down again.

The show had begun!

And Gravyhead had lost the key.

Dad was standing beside him, muttering, whilst the first act jumbled nervously behind him.

'Come on, come on! We've got to get started!'

'Don't panic. Keep your shirt on. It must be around here somewhere. All I've got to do is find it.'

'Look under the light!' said some smart Alec.

'Keep your own shirt on!' said another.

'Let's go around the front!' goaded a third.

Gravyhead scrabbled on the path, his knees in a puddle, with the key dangling below his nose, like a pygmy ice cream cone.

'There it is! Give it to me! Quickly!'

That was Dad, trying to keep his jokes warm.

He wrenched open the door and disappeared on stage, the drums rolled, and he launched into his routine. I could just hear it, through my burning ears.

'Good evening, ladies and gentlemen!'

They all yelled back at him various things.

'Did you hear about the man who tried to tell us he came from Wales?'

Everybody said they hadn't.

'I knew he was a liar straight away. And do you know how I knew he was a liar straight away?'

Everybody said they didn't.

'I knew straight away that he wasn't from Wales because he had never heard of a harpoon!!'

For some reason everybody laughed. They shouldn't have done that because they'd only encourage him. And they did, and the next one was even worse.

'How do dogs like their trees?' he asked.

'We don't know. How do dogs like their trees?' asked some fool in the audience.

That nearly threw Dad and I thought he'd forgotten the answer. Not that it'd be funny, anyway.

'They like their trees with plenty of bark!!' shouted Dad, remembering the punch line in the nick of time.

I suppose they laughed because he was so thin.

'And now, ladies and gentlemen,' said Dad, and I could see him smiling even out the back, 'and now I'm pleased to present to you, for the first time on any stage anywhere, especially in Niamong, our first act, the Fabulous Famous Rawlinnson Knuckle Dancers!!!'

The piano banged into a marching tune, echoed by Mr Manderson's drums, and the Rawlinnsons paraded on, with me close behind so I didn't miss seeing them.

Mr Rawlinnson was dressed in a moth-eaten kangaroo skin, a nappy tied somehow around where nappies are supposed to go. He hopped, more or less, and skipped, less or more, onto the stage, juggling a pair of knuckles from his left hand knuckles to his right hand.

Behind him came Mrs Rawlinnson, in what must have been her grandmother's wedding dress. She was pushing a pram which had Tim Rawlinnson in it, dressed as a baby even though he hadn't been one for about twenty years. He had a big knuckle in his mouth, which matched the ones his mother was wearing around her neck, and he waved his fist at the audience. The other two Rawlinnson boys went on last, dressed only in nappies and knuckles. In fact I think their nappies *were* knuckles because they made a lot of noise as the boys danced around, giving a little jump and a yelp every now and then when the knuckles crashed together when and where they weren't expecting it.

I couldn't see properly but everybody was laughing their head off, and I could hear what must've been hundreds of knuckles crashing onto the floor. The Rawlinnsons kept on slipping over and getting up as the music went faster and faster and the drums thrashed louder and louder until there was a huge bang as the Rawlinnsons fell off the stage into a pile of kerosene tins they'd put there before the show.

Applause rocked the hall as the curtains closed and Dad went out to announce the next act.

'Thank you The Rawlinnsons! I can see that you were really knuckling down tonight!' Where does he get these things from?! 'Did you hear about the love sick owl, caught in a storm so bad, the winds so strong, and the rain so heavy, that all he could do was sit on his branch in the old dead tree and say over and over again, "Too-wet-to-woo, too-wet-to-woo, too-wet-to-woo!'

Again everybody laughed. Maybe you had to be grownup. Then he was off again.

'Did you hear why all the cars drive so slowly in Moscow, and why they hardly ever get anywhere?'

Everybody said they hadn't a clue, and as far as I was concerned I didn't care a bit that I wasn't Sherlock Holmes or Dr Livingstone.

'All the cars drive so slowly because all the traffic lights are red!' he yelled.

Well, so is the newspaper but that doesn't stop you reading it quickly if you want to. When will he start telling jokes that make sense?

The next act was Katie and Meaghan playing a duet on the piano, and then it went back to the jokes.

'Did you hear about the man who wanted to commit suicide in a completely new way?' he cried. I wondered if there'd be anyone left in the audience for *my* play.

'He thought and thought about it, then one day he got it. He caught a train down to Melbourne, rushed into the Indian restaurant, and committed hurry curry!!'

I didn't see that diving into a bowl of curry and rice would be too much of a problem for anyone, but at least it was funnier than a koala taking off its clothes in the desert.

'And now, ladies and gentlemen, something rather special. I'm very proud to introduce the next item, and to tell you that it was written by Lissie Pendle!!'

Everybody cheered and whistled. They probably thought it was going to be about a pencil and be called The Thin Man or something.

'My daughter,' and I could see Dad puffing up as he used to do when Bill was little, before the car episode, 'my daughter has written a play for you. It's really a sketch, but how can you have a sketch without any drawings!!' He laughed his head off for a few seconds, even though I'd thought of it first.

'Lissie's play is called *Mr Fixit Motors*, and I think it's all about *your* garage, Jack!' he laughed, looking at someone in the audience. Actually it was set in Melbourne, where I'd been for a holiday once.

'Ladies and gentlemen! *Mr Fixit Motors*, by Lissie Pendle!!'

I'll write out the play properly here, so that you'll know that it's a proper play, but I'll put in extra bits to help you know what's going on. Don't forget that it's very funny. And it starts just over the page.

Mr Fixit Motors

Characters

Jones   a well-to-do businessman, with lots of money, played by Robbie

Gravystein   who thinks he's funny, played by Jingo

Hassle   his young assistant, who should've been played by Topsy Templeton, but who was played by Jemmy

Scene One

In front of the curtain, with the lights out. (This is called 'tabs,' but that looks too much like stab.)

A telephone rings off stage. Ring ring Ring ring Ring ring (A few too many rings happened here because Gravyhead lost the key again)

Voice: (Shouting through the curtains because the off-stage microphone had been pulled out of its socket a minute before and it was too dark back there to find where to put it.)

Good morning. Mr Fixit Motors. Thank you for your call and we hope you have a nice day.

Jones: (Also shouting through the curtains, for the same reason)

Hello, hello. Is that Mr Gravystein?

Gravy: Shtein! Shtein! (You have to say it that way, because it's a German word)

Jones: Shtein? I'm ringing about my car, not beer mugs!

(Steins are German beer mugs. Dad's got one on the mantelpiece, full of dust. I think he bought it in Ballargo.)

Gravy: No no no no. My name is Gravyshtein!

Jones: Oh. I do beg your pardon, Mr Gravy, er...stein...shtein! Now, about my car...

(Don't forget that all this is happening behind the curtain and there's still no microphone.)

Gravy: Car? Yes, we have lots of cars here. Which one do you want?

(I forgot to tell you that he was a German
migrant, so you have to get the accent
right in your mind.)

Jones: My car, Mr Gravy...er...shtein. I left it last
week.

(Weren't Jingo and Robbie acting well!)

Gravy: Last week....?

Jones: Yes. It's red...

Gravy: Red? With number plates?

Jones: Of course it has number plates!

Gravy: Ah, I remember the one. A silver Porsche.

Jones: Red!

Gravy: We have no red Porsches! Only silver
ones. Only one silver one.

Jones: Not a Porsche! I wanted new covers on
the pedals.

Gravy: Pedals?! Are you a drug pusher!?

Jones: Mr Gravystein...

Gravy: Shstein!

Jones: Shstein!! You were fixing the pedals in my
car! You know, pedals you put your feet
on! You promised you'd fix them straight
away!

Gravy:	Fix them? No no. We are Fix It. Mr Fix It Motors. We fix IT, not them!
Jones:	It was only a little job, Mr Fix It...er...Gravyshstein. It was supposed to be ready three days ago! Do I have to report you to the police to get my car fixed?!
Gravy:	Police?! Now I remember. You brought in a red car!
Jones:	Yes!
Gravy:	A mini.
Jones:	Yes! With number plates! And wheels! And bumper bars! Yes, and pedals! (That bit was really good, wasn't it!)
Gravy:	Pedals? You want them fixed?
Jones:	YES! You said they'd be fixed three days ago...
Gravy:	They're fixed.
Jones:	You promised me they'd be fixed by Tuesday! You...fixed?
Gravy:	Fixed.
Jones:	You mean...repaired, mended, made-like-new, FIXED?

Gravy:	Fixed. That's our business. Mr Fixit.
Jones:	I know. Fixed. (Robbie put on his most suspicious voice) Does that mean that I can pick it up today?
Gravy:	Yes.
Jones:	I can leave work early and catch the tram out and walk down to your garage and PICK UP MY CAR, today?
Gravy:	Yes.
Jones:	Don't hang up!

Scene Two

The curtains open. There is a pool of light, centre stage, right. Small, worn- out desk, littered with papers. Gravystein is sitting at the desk, the phone to his ear, an unlit cigarette in his mouth. (I don't know where Jingo got that from – it wasn't in the script.)

Gravy:	Hassle! Come here and hold this phone. I need to go out the back for a minute. (All the boys in the audience laughed at that, but I don't know why.)
Hassle:	Who is it? (That was Jemmy)

Gravy:	A customer. He said to hang on, but I can't hang on any longer. (He goes off, quickly,) (Jones comes on, mopping his brow)
Jones:	Mr Gravystein?
Hassle:	It's shstein. Gravyshstein.
Jones:	Shstein. I've come for my car.
Hassle:	Just a moment. I'm on the phone.
Jones:	That's me!
Hassle:	Sorry?
Jones:	That's me on the phone!
Hassle:	No, I'm holding on to a customer, and you're here. (You can see what I meant about Topsy Templeton)
Jones:	Of course I'm here, because I'm not there!
Hassle:	I can see that. Do you take me for a fool?
Jones:	Mr Gravystein...
Hassle:	Shstein! And it's Hassle.
Jones:	I'm not hassling you, Mr Shstein...
Hassle:	Mr Gravyshstein...I'm hassled...I mean I'm Hassle! (Enter Gravystein)

Gravy:	You still hangin' on, Hassle?
Hassle:	He's not there!
Jones:	It's me!
Gravy:	Who are you?
Jones:	I'm Jones. Who are you?
Gravy:	Gravystein...
Hassle:	Shstein!
Jones:	Shstein.
Gravy:	Shstein.
Jones:	Mr Fixit? Then who's this?
Gravy:	My apprentice, Hassle.
	(Hassle goes to hang up the phone.)
	Don't, Hassle!
Hassle:	It's not a hassle. There's no one there.
Jones:	I'm here, for Pete's sake! You two have the brains of old bananas – two skins filled with useless pulp!
Gravy:	Now now. Who are you calling pulp?! And who's this Pete feller?
Jones:	I've come about my car!
	(You can tell that he was getting very excited, can't you?)

Gravy:	Car? Yes, we have lots of cars here. Which one do you want?
Jones:	Don't start that again! My red car with the pedals!
Gravy:	All cars've got pedals.
Jones:	I know that, you fool! You said it was ready and I could pick it up today!
Gravy:	I did? Hassle, duck out and see if we've got that red car ready. Red-y - get it?! (Hassle goes off) You're car isn't one of those new ones put out by the American soft drink company, is it?
Jones:	Soft drink company? Soft drink companies don't make cars!
Gravy:	This one does. Haven't you heard of the Coca Corolla? (Hassle comes back on, carrying a small car part. He whispers in Gravystein's ear, discussing a problem.) OK, OK, get on with it! (Hassle exits)
Jones:	What was that all about?

Gravy:	It seems that were having a small problem with your car.
Jones:	But you said it was ready!
Gravy:	Won't be a moment. He's a great apprentice. Never forgets anything, you know. Though sometimes he takes a darn long time remembering.
	(Hassle returns, carrying a larger piece of a car. He and Gravystein have another long whisper, arms going everywhere)
	All right, all right. Just get it fixed.
	(Hassle exits)
Jones:	What is going on? I only wanted new caps on the pedals.
Gravy:	**Just a small problem. Say, did you hear about the dumb guy who was so dumb that he thought a locomotive was a crazy reason?**
Jones:	I want my car!
	(Hassle enters, juggling several large pieces of machinery and a fan belt.)
	What's this?! What's he doing to my car!!?

	(Hassle and Gravystein get into a deep conversation)
	Gravystein...!
Gravy:	(looking up) Shtein, shtein.
Jones:	You said three days. I've given you five! You said it was ready. You said I could pick it up today! I left work early and lost half a day's pay! I caught a tram out and I walked miles down here and when I get here I find a mess of bits and pieces and two hopeless so-called mechanics with the brainpower of an EIGHTEENTH CENTURY DONKEY!!!
Gravy:	That'd be dead by now.
Jones:	That's what I meant! I WANT MY CAR!!!
Gravy:	OK, OK OK all right all right!
	(He and Hassle rush off)
	(Gravystein returns)
	Here it is!
	(And Hassle comes on, riding in a child's peddle car!)
	(And all the lights went out, because that was the end.)

176

Everybody stamped and cheered and whistled. They all stood up and shouted 'Pendle Pendle Pendle.' Dad grabbed my hand and pulled me out to bow with Jingo and Jemmy and Robbie. We bowed and smiled and I held Jingo's and Jemmy's hands, and forgot all about the bush dance.

I don't remember any of the other acts that night, but I knew that I'd got it.

I'd got Pendle Power!

10

Lost Brother

...where I made a friend.

I'd finally worked it out. It'd been puzzling me all my life, ever since I'd first learnt how to puzzle.

Why didn't Father Christmas ever give Mum and Dad presents at Christmas time?

I'd talked about it with all the kids at school, but most of them didn't care, or else they said they didn't believe in Father Christmas. As long as the presents kept coming at the end of each year it didn't worry them.

Jemmy and Jingo said that it was because parents were too old, and what would they do with toys anyway.

Lonie thought that it was because Father Christmas just wouldn't have time to make all the extra things, and Mother Christmas, if there was one, would've been flat out keeping Father Christmas fat, cooking and all that, so she wouldn't have had time, either.

Scratcher said that it was because his Mum and Dad were never home on Christmas Eve, and that Father Christmas wouldn't be allowed in the Lalor's Arms.

The McPhees said that Father Christmas didn't come to any of them, but that didn't surprise us – how could he get through the smell? And even if he did, the ferrets'd scare off the reindeer.

And Geoff, who was going to be a retired engineer one day, said that sleighs couldn't get off the ground at the North Pole because the snow would be too hard or too soft.

No, the reason was simple. You've probably noticed this yourself – your parents never give you any presents: they always rely on Father Christmas to give them to you. Even rich parents let Father Christmas do all the work, so Father Christmas said to himself, or to Mother Christmas if there was one, and if she was there at the time, 'Why should I go to all the bother of making lots of presents for all the millions and squillions of parents when they're too stingy to give presents to their own lovely children? I'll just teach them a lesson and not give them any, and see how they like that. When they wake up to themselves and realise how mean and selfish they've been all these years, and start giving their children presents again, so that the kids get two lots of presents, then I might think about giving them some, if they're very good during the year, that is.'

And I think Father Christmas was right.

He was especially right this year, because he brought us a tent. A big tent, big enough for all of us, and so we decided to go camping. Before the tent arrived Dad had been talking about us going down to Melbourne to stay with Nan for a week or so, but after it'd come we all decided that we ought to try it out with a good camp.

Mum wasn't all that keen on camping in a tent, with snakes and frogs creeping under the walls, but Dad said it would be good, and Father Christmas must've heard him.

It had white sides and a green roof. There was a thick pole to go up the middle, to hold up the roof, and thinner and shorter poles for the corners and in between. All the poles were made up of two halves which you joined together when you were putting up the tent. Each pole except the middle one had a long rope with it, and you put one end of the rope around a spike on the top of the pole and tied the other end on to a tent peg in the ground. Then the tent stood up.

Getting ready for a camp takes a lot of time: there are so many things to do and you have to try to keep Bill out of the way at the same time.

On the day before we were leaving Bill spent half a day trying to work out which half of an orange had the more juice in it – the part with the stem, where it hung from the tree, or the other half. I said it'd be the other half, because the juice would have to go towards the bottom, but he wouldn't listen. He said the juice came out of the tree, through the stem, so it'd be up the top. I said that was probably true for him but not for oranges. Anyway, he had to find out, with all our oranges.

Afterwards he spent the rest of the day in the toilet, and he still didn't know the answer.

We drove out to Emu Point for our camp, on the lake which was not all that far from Niamong. It was a rather special lake, not at all like the ones at Melbourne or San Francisco or those other places. This one was really two lakes, one in summer and a different one in winter, or some winters, anyway. Most of the time it was dry and you could walk all over it, and play with the old tyres and wheels and things, and even climb up hills and down valleys. Or you could light a fire and have a barbecue or a picnic. In winter, if there'd been plenty of rain for once, it'd fill up, or try hard to fill up if there hadn't been a lot of rain. Then the wildflowers would come out all over the place, making it look like a huge puddle with splashes of coloured paint all around it. And you had to watch out for the quicksand along the shore.

Right at the end of the point was a nice flat piece of ground. Lots of great big red gums were dotted about, shading the grass. A pair of rosellas had made a nest in a hollow broken branch high up in the tree, and little honeyeaters twittered amongst the leaves, until they saw Bill, then they twittered off somewhere else.

We pitched our tent a bit away from the trees, just in case one of the rotten branches broke off in the middle of the night and fell on my rotten little brother when he'd finally gone to sleep.

Dad dug a trench for our fire, and another one further away, in the trees, for when you wanted to go (this one had a hessian wall around it so nobody could see you, unless the sun was shining along the ground. It's too em-barrassing to tell you any more about that place or what you had to do in it, and how you did it, so you'll just have to make it up yourself: after all, why should I have to do everything in this story?).

Other people were camping at Emu Point, too, which was good, because I didn't want to have to play with Bill all the time. In fact I didn't want to play with him at all but Mum and Dad always got in a rage when I said that so I usually did something with him to keep them quiet.

After we'd set up the camp Bill went down to the beach to look at the quicksand and I headed around to the other side of the point to see if there was anyone there my age. When you're on a holiday somewhere you have to make friends very quickly or it's too late and you have to go home after a terrible torturing time with your brother.

There was a girl paddling in the water. I was in luck. I knew it was a girl, even though she had her back to me, because she had nice longish hair and seemed to know what she was doing. Boys never know what they're doing: they just do it and hope for the best.

'Hello,' I said. I could've said 'G'day' but I didn't think she was that sort of person.

'Hello,' she said, turning to me and smiling. I was right. It's very important to use the right word.

'Are you having a holiday?' I asked. I knew that she wasn't there to build a house but it's polite to ask a new person something that you know that they know the answer to.

'Yes,' she said, without any trouble, and pointed over her shoulder to somewhere.

'Your Mum and Dad here?' I asked.

'Yes,' she said, 'and my brother.'

We were friends, quick as lightning.

'My brother's here, too,' I said, and she knew we were friends. 'Have you been here long?'

'A couple of days. We live in Kyneton.'

'My aunt lives in Kyneton,' I said. 'The one with nine fingers.'

'Nine fingers?'

'Well, it's really seven fingers, and two thumbs. No one else knows except me. And her,' I said.

'Oh," she said, splashing the water a bit and giving a little fish a fright. The extra talking mark meant that she was trying to remember whether she had any aunts with only nine fingers, counting the thumbs.

'She's not really an aunt,' I said, and I could see that she rubbed out the extra talking mark. If she hadn't been my friend I would've made her keep it there.

'My great-grandfather or something used to be the Pound Keeper at Heathcote,' she said. 'He's buried there.'

'Did he look after all the money?' I asked – I hadn't noticed the capital P on Pound Keeper.

'No, he looked after animals that strayed,' she said, not making me look silly, and I thought of Bill for some reason. 'People had to pay to get them out. I suppose they had to pay a pound or something.'

The holiday was starting to get on a bit so I thought I'd better ask her what I really wanted to ask. It hadn't been the right time up until then.

'What's your name?' I said, looking over towards our camp.

She didn't say anything, and I thought that I must've asked her a bit too soon.

'Mine's Liss,' I said. 'I'm not all that keen on it but I'm stuck with it, at least till I'm grown up.' I nearly told her about Jingo and me getting married then, but as I hadn't really talked to him about it yet I thought I'd better not.

'It's MG,' she said, and I didn't know what she was talking about. 'I like being called that,' she said. I wondered if I should call myself L, but I thought that if I did I might go to the wrong place when I died.

'Names are funny things,' she said. 'Your parents give them to you without asking whether they're the ones you really want. They're ones that *they* really want, or else they couldn't think of anything else, or else they have to call you that or a rich aunt won't leave them any money when she dies.'

With all this dying going on I started thinking of the stains Bill always left on the tablecloth at home.

'If you're not careful,' she said, 'you might start to look like your name. That's all right if you like your name, but not if you don't. It's the same with dogs.'

I didn't really know what she was talking about now (was she really a little grown-up?), but it made me sad again about Brissy.

Just then I heard Mum calling. The sun was starting to get down behind the trees and the mossies were starting to get up my skirt.

'You going to be here long?'

'About a week.'

'So'm I.'

'I might see you tomorrow, then.'

'Might.'

She went off along the beach, squelching in the mud, and I went back through the trees to our camp.

Dad was standing by the fire. He had on one of his half smug smiles – I wasn't sure which one, until I got closer to the fire and saw the frying pan, and smelt the delicious smell. He'd caught some fish in the lake. Lots of times he'd boasted about when he was a small boy in Albany, when he'd caught about fifty-eight herrings off the jetty. I wasn't too interested in that, but this was different.

My mouth began to water. Dad's smile was now all smug and I hadn't the heart to tell him what other words you could make out of smug. It wouldn't've been the right time, either, if I wanted my share of fresh-fried fish.

'I caught them,' he said, puffing up.

I knew that the fish must've helped a bit, or we'd have been eating baked beans.

'I told you I could catch fish. Remember the herrings in Albany?'

'They look delicious, Dad. When're we having them?'

'Right now! The table's laid and the others are waiting in the tent. Come on!'

He scooped up the frying pan and we went in a short but proud procession to the dinner table. Hot fish and hot chips! And a few peas, but I don't like that word very much. It was the best meal I'd ever had, with the pressure lamp hissing from a hook on the pole, and the sounds of birds squawking into their sleeping perches.

*****

'Can we go over to Green Island today please Mum?'

Bill was talking before the birds had started their squawking for the new day.

'Can I Mum? Mum! Dad?'

Something that sounded like 'I'll see' mumbled from one of the sleeping bags.

Good! When parents say 'I'll see' it means that you've got them. It doesn't matter what they say later, or what happens: they *have* to let you do whatever they said they'd see about, because they'd said. This is one of the main rules of managing parents. Even Bill knows that one.

He scrambled out of his sleeping bag and went outside.

He was still in yesterday's clothes.

'Don t forget to do it in the hessian shelter!' I called. He would've gone in the bushes.

I quickly got dressed in my sleeping bag so he wouldn't see me, except for my shoes, and went outside. The sun was coming up over the low hills on the other side of the lake, making a sort of wavy golden path on the water. A mob of white cockatoos flew along the far shore, screeching like Mrs Armstrong's cat that day when Petchie chased it up the lamp post, and a few sheep were fleecing round a paddock like bundles of woolly jumpers.

It was going to be a beautiful day, just right for exploring the island.

There were still some warm coals in the fire so I collected dry grass and small twigs and put these on the coals. A few puffs and the fire was going again, and bigger bits of wood finished it off.

I took Mum and Dad a mug of tea each, to have before they properly woke up, and to help them get into a good mood so they wouldn't forget about Green Island.

Along the shore of the lake was an old boat shed, half in and half out of the water. Its doors had more or less fallen off and the paint was stripping off the walls like bark off a tree trunk. Inside was a long brown wooden rowing boat. It belonged to one of the farmers who lived near the lake and he let campers use it as long as they were careful. We were going to borrow it to row out to the island.

Mum wasn't too keen about the whole idea but Dad said it'd be all right because they'd be able to see us all the way, and it wasn't far out to the island anyway.

We packed our lunch in a waterproof bag and piled into the boat, Bill in the stern and me in the middle – I was going to be the rower.

'Now you be careful, both of you,' said Mum. 'Especially you, Bill. No funny business.'

Why was she always worried about him? What about me? If the boat sank I'd be in the water, too. I suppose it was because he was a boy, and born stupid.

'Yes, Mum,' we both said. You have to say that, don't you, or you'd never be allowed to go anywhere on your own. I think that I probably meant it, but I doubt if Bill did. He just said things to keep his voice awake.

Off we paddled, with the sun on my back and a little breeze keeping us cool. Bill sat all the way, trailing his hand over the back until I told him that a fish might bite off his fingers. It hardly took any time to reach the island

and we had a good explore, Bill chasing the finches and butterflies and falling over every few minutes.

We had our picnic lunch on the other side of the island, under a stunted tree with its roots wriggling across the ground into the water. Then we walked right around the island, jumping over old tree trunks and stumps, and then we walked around again, the other way. Just as we arrived back at the boat I saw Mum waving that it was time to come back. If we'd been on the other side it wouldn't have mattered, but she knew that I'd seen her, so we had to go. I climbed into the boat and Bill pushed us off, hopping wetly in before I started rowing.

Suddenly Bill snatched the oars from me and tried to row. He must have been planning that all the time. One oar went over the side. I jumped up and tried to catch it and kicked the other one over the side, too. Unfortunately Bill was still holding on to that one and he went over after the oars. I thought of leaving him there but I knew that I'd probably get into trouble if I did, so I jumped into the water and swam towards him. At the same time I saw Dad dive in from the shore and Mum run up the beach to somewhere.

The water was freezing but I hardly noticed as I was so worried about Bill, but when I got to him he was laughing his head off.

'Do that again Liss! That was great fun! How'd you do it, Liss?'

He was just hanging from the oar like a bat from a branch, spurting water and kicking his feet. I thought I was being a hero, or at least a heroine, and here he was having the time of his life!

Brothers make you sick, and Dad wasn't too pleased when he finally arrived, to find us playing hide and seek with the boat and the two oars. We dragged him into the boat and laid him down in the bottom to get his breath back and warm up. We shouldn't have done that, because as soon as he was warmed up he warmed up our bottoms, but not too much, and everything turned out all right because Mum had made us a mug of hot cocoa and warmed up some fresh clothes.

Bill wandered off up the beach and I went around to find MG.

***

We walked along the beach together, away from the camp. Around that side the water was farther from the shore than on our side; the ground was very flat and a bit muddy, with bulrushes sticking up in the air waiting for a bull to rush by.

I kept a pretty sharp eye out for bulls, because I wasn't all that keen on them any more, and it'd be hard running away through the mud.

'I saved Bill. From drowning.' There's not much harm in letting someone know you're brave, as long as it doesn't come out as a boast.

'Why?' said MG.

She was getting me back for the nine fingers.

'He'd fallen in the water. Out of the boat.' I knew that it wasn't really a very good reason, but he *was* my brother. Blood's thicker than water, even when it's made out of tomato sauce.

'I'd've left him, if he'd been my brother.'

'So would I,' I said, but I wasn't quite sure which brother we were talking about.

'Do you know why they're called 'grown-ups?' she said. 'It's because they're always groaning: 'Why did you do that?' and 'When are you going to stop doing that?' and 'I'm fed up with you lying around in your messy room all day'.

I knew what she meant. From now on I'd call them groan-ups, too.

'What's your best thing at school?' I asked, to get her thinking about something else.

'Running.'

'Running? That's one of my favourite things, too!'

'Running away from school,' she said. 'That's the best thing at my school.'

'We've got Mr Braden at our school.'

'Mr Braden!? Wow! You poor thing!'

I hadn't realised that everybody knew about him, even down in Kyneton.

'Oh, he's not too bad,' I said, shrugging my shoulders bravely and looking up at the sky, wondering if Halley's Comet was just a story the older people told.

'I'm a good runner,' she said. 'Want a race?'

So we went for a race around the lake, except that it was so far that we had to walk most of the way and didn't get back to camp till the sun was down on the tops of the trees.

'Where've you been!' said the first groan-up we saw. It was Mum, and she didn't look quite right. 'Have you seen Bill? He hasn't come back. He's been gone for ages!'

So'd we, but that didn't seem to matter so much.

'Go around to the other camps and see if he's playing with anyone.'

That's one of those things about parents: they can't see when you've had enough and you just want to lie down or read a book or something. They just tell you to go off and find your brother. I'd already saved him once – why couldn't someone else go?

MG and I walked off through the other camps, calling to him whenever no one was looking at us. But he wasn't anywhere. Even the boat shed was empty, except for the boat. I could see that Mum was really worried when we got back to our camp, and so was Dad.

'We'd better go and look for him. I'll ask the other people if they'll help.'

This was starting to get exciting. If he was really lost we might get in the newspaper.

Pretty soon all the groan-ups were outside our tent, looking important and wondering whether their tea would stay hot till they got back.

'He's probably not far away,' said Dad. 'Let's all spread along the shore and then walk inland. We'll soon find him.'

He looked at Mum when he said that, and she sniffed a bit. I thought that Bill'd probably gone to sleep under a grass tree or something. Instead of going out looking for him we should just make the cooking smells blow in the right direction. MG and I went off towards the setting sun, shouting his name every few minutes and kicking any grass trees that we came across.

My voice began to get sore so I stopped shouting too much. So did MG. Tea trees grew on the sandy hills and we struggled through these, panting up the slopes. We shouldn't've gone for that run. We were so tired. We sat down in a little valley, then we lay down in the little valley. There's nothing like a good lie down, especially when you're looking for little brothers.

'Aren't brothers stupid,' said MG.

I was too tired to answer, but everyone knew that little brothers were stupid, so it didn't matter, and she hadn't used a question mark, anyway.

'Trust them to get lost,' she said. 'What a dumb thing to do.'

Bill wasn't really all that dumb. In fact I could only remember him being dumb when he was fast asleep. All the rest of the time he was talking, even when he was eating.

'Why can't boys be like girls?' she said.

I'd always thought that, too, except for Jingo. And Jemmy.

'We wouldn't have gone off and got lost,' she said. 'We have to do the finding.'

'He's probably back at camp by now,' I said. 'Tucking into bread and Vegemite.'

'Let's go back,' said MG. 'We can't stay out here all night.'

All night! Suddenly we saw that the sun'd gone down. The valley was black and splotchy, and quiet.

Quite quiet, which are two words with the same letters, and one of them's spooky.

'Which way do we go?'

MG looked around.

'That way.'

'I think it's this way.'

'No, down there,' said MG, pointing the other way to the way she'd said before.

'We came up this little valley, then we sat down here,' I said.

'No, we came up that little valley, and sat over there.'

We decided to walk to the top of the hill to see if we could work out which was the right way to go.

The top of the hill was full of trees, and it was darker than anywhere else, so we went back down again and nearly fell into a creek. We'd gone down a different way.

'The creek must go into the lake,' said MG. 'Let's follow it. Well soon be home.'

That made a lot of sense to me, but the water soon dried up at a flat spot where lots of little valleys went off in different directions.

'I'm too tired to keep on.'

'Me, too.'

We sat down again, huddling together because it was getting very cold.

'Do you think we should keep on shouting?' I asked.

'No. They'd think that we were lost.'

'I meant for Bill,' I said, thinking about that just in time.

'Oh. Yes, that'd be all right.'

So we shouted and shouted. And shouted. Pretty soon a couple of horses were stuck in our throats and we couldn't shout any more. The wind was making funny noises that weren't funny in the trees and black clouds kept on covering the moon. I decided that sun shadows were nice but moon shadows would've looked better in the daytime.

'Do you think we should stay here for a while?'

'Yes. We might trip over something and hurt ourselves in the dark.'

I put my arm around MG, to keep her warm. Stars raced between the clouds and clouds kept on jumping into the moon's mouth, making her go black in the face. I shivered and MG put her arm around me, to keep me warm, too.

Then I heard a faint shouting.

'They're still looking for Bill!' I yelled. We jumped up and coughed the horses out of our throats.

'Bill! Bill! Bill!' we shouted. A light splashed through the trees along one of the valleys. 'Bill! Bill! Dad!!'

'Liss! Where are you?'

It was Dad!

'Over here! In this valley! On the flat!'

'We're looking for Bill,' yelled MG.

Dad and MG's father ran into the clearing, lanterns laughing away the shadows.

'We've been looking everywhere for *you*!'

'We were looking for Bill.'

'We found him hours ago. He was asleep under a grass tree!'

I knew it. Boys are so stupid.

'You were good girls staying in one place. We mightn't have found you for days if you'd wandered around.'

'We weren't lost, Dad. We just got a bit tired, and the sun went down.'

'Oh. Well, come on. We'll get you back to camp for a hot drink.'

Pretty soon there were two piggybacks in operation and after only about a million bounces we were in front of our campfire. Mum pretended to be angry as she boiled the milk for some cocoa and made some hot buttered toast with honey. I snuggled onto Dad's lap and started to think warm and sleepy thoughts.

'Dad. Can you like someone as well as love them?'

Dad was quiet for a bit.

'You can like someone without loving them, and you can probably love them without liking them sometimes, or you can love them and like them. Just as Mum and I like you and love you.'

'Me too,' I said. Most of the time.

Mum's stomach rumbled quietly next to me, and I knew that I was safe.

11

Crutches

...where I nearly put my foot in it.

'Foul! That's a foul!'

'It wasn't!'

'It was, Scratcher! That was a foul!'

'No, it wasn't! There aren't any fouls in cricket!' he yelled, as three hens and a rooster ran across the pitch.

'You're not allowed to bowl with your arm bent!'

'I haven't got a bowl! So how could it be bent!'

'I saw you throw it! You chucked the ball! You didn't bowl it!'

'I didn't, and you're out!'

'I'm not. You can't go out on a foul!'

'You are, and I told you there aren't any fouls in cricket. That's baseball. You're out, and I'm in.'

'It was a no ball! And I'm not out! I'm still in! You're a cheat, Scratcher!'

The whole world went still when one of the McPhees said that. It was like Mr Braden coming to your birthday party. Scratcher'd been bowling at the McPhees, which meant that he'd been bowling into the wind, and they'd been in for hours. It didn't matter how fast you bowled – the ball just seemed to slow down when it got near them, and they smashed it into the gully or the creek or into the scrub. If you did tricky spinners the ball always turned away from the stumps, and they smashed it into the scrub or the gully or the creek. We were sick of chasing the ball everywhere. Even Petchie had decided to lie down under a peppercorn tree and let her tongue turn the dust into mud.

'I'm dobbin' on ya,' said one of the McPhees, but he didn't use an exclamation mark, so I knew that he knew that he was in trouble. My foot stamped itself on the ground a few times and I let fly at him.

'They should send you on a camp for upper-privileged kids!' I yelled.

'Who asked you!' yelled the other McPhee.

'I wasn't speaking to you when I was yelling!' I yelled. 'McPhew!'

That one was wasted on them because they didn't know what it meant. They'd probably faint if they ever went into a houseful of clean people.

'Come on! We're goin' home! We're not playin' with cheats and girls!'

'Good riddance to bad rubbish!' the rest of us yelled, glad that we'd finally got both McPhees out. And we didn't have to bowl them out, so I suppose it was a no ball after all.

It'd been a good game up until when the McPhees had gone in to bat. I could bowl everybody else out, with my fast leg breaks, even Jingo, and I scored nearly as many runs as he did, but the McPhees were another kettle of fish, in fact a kettle of fish that'd been out in the sun for about two weeks.

Mrs Macleod's shop was nice and cool when we went into buy an ice block and see what she'd been eating for her afternoon tea. Jemmy had a red one, Jingo had a green one, Scratcher had a yellow one, and I had one with lots of bits of chopped-up fruit in it which felt funny in my mouth as I ate it – hard and soft and melty and cold all at the same time. It was just the right thing after the McPhees, making my nose go numb.

We all spent quite a bit of time licking our ice blocks so that we could have a good look at the jars of lollies, and so that the lollies could get a good look at us, because we were going to look after them all properly. One day. We hoped.

It's a funny thing about eating and drinking – you do it through your head. I can't quite work out why we're made that way. It makes a lot of sense to have your eyes up there (so that you can get a good view and all that), and the same with your ears. Even your nose, except that a longer neck would be useful sometimes. But it doesn't seem right to have your mouth up there. It's such a long way from your stomach. Why isn't your mouth on the outside of your stomach? You wouldn't need to swallow all the food, or get it caught in your throat if it was fish bones, and you'd never have to clean your teeth. And if they didn't cut off your cord just after you were born you could use it as a straw, and be able to drink, eat, and talk at the same time. Bill wouldn't want to leave the dinner table.

Outside in the main street things had begun to happen since we'd gone in for our ice blocks. A lot of men were out there, standing in the backs of utes and climbing up ladders or standing on boxes, talking and shouting as they strung coloured light globes along the shop verandahs. Others were putting a great big banner right across the street from the shops to one of the palm trees on the other side. It was so big that I thought it'd probably blow away like a galleon if the wind got too strong, which would give the sparrows a bit of a fright. And Graveyhead, too, if he was coming out of the Lalor's Arms at the wrong time.

'What's going on? What are they doing that for?' said Jemmy, licking the last bit of ice block cone off the end of his nose.

'It's for the festival,' I said. 'Dad told me about it.'

'What's a vestibule, Liss?' asked Scratcher, who once thought that an eisteddfod had something to do with ice.

'Not a vestibule! That's in a church. Festival. Where you have fun and fairy floss and stuff.'

'Oh. Like the Show.'

'Yes, except that there aren't any animals. Especially bulls,' said Jemmy, looking at me.

WELCOME TO NIAMONG it said, which didn't seem all that exciting to us. Who'd want to come to Niamong? Most people couldn't even say it properly —

whenever Mrs Foster came up from Melbourne she always called it Nearmong, and I wondered where Farmong was.

But then we noticed that Scratcher's father and Mr Brister were hanging up another huge banner a bit further down the street, and that one was much more interesting because it told us what was happening.

FIRST ANNUAL DUST FESTIVAL

Dust festival?!

Suddenly everyone up a ladder or on a box or in the back of a ute climbed down and jumped off and leapt out of whatever they were up, on, or in and raced into the shops, shouting something.

We turned and looked up the road, and saw why we were having a dust festival. A great cloud of red dust was rolling over the countryside towards the town, turning the sun down low and making the birds in the palm trees twitter and twotter, getting ready for bed. We couldn't take our eyes off it – it was amazing.

I think it was Mr Houghton who grabbed us and stuffed us through the door of one of the shops. We could hardly see anything, even with our noses pressed against the windowpanes. Bits of newspaper tumbled down the street, red all over, and leaves, and dust. In no time at all it'd seeped through the cracks and we were sneezing our heads off, wondering if there'd be any hairs left to keep out the germs in winter. What was Bill doing – he was probably hiding under his bedclothes.

After a while it started to get lighter again, and then it was sunny. And then I realised we'd been sheltering in Mrs Armstrong's shop! All those lovely lollies lying lonely in their jars, sticking to each other for company when we'd gladly have helped them out, and in! If we'd known where we were.

The men all went for a long walk and brought back the banners from the saleyards, where they'd sailed to in the wind, and fixed them up again.

'Where's all the dust gone?'

'To Melbourne. And it serves them right.'

On the day of the opening of the festival the town was fuller than Bill's stomach on his birthday. All the coloured lights were on, even though it wasn't nighttime, and the banners flapped in the dust thrown up by the cars and utes. People had set up stalls under the palms and peppercorns opposite the shops and were selling all sorts of things. The Bowers had their hot dogs again and Mrs

Ray had decided that she could sell her lemonade twice a year, seeing that it was a special occasion.

Mrs Gordon had brought up some of her spicy crust pies from Melbourne, Mrs Boulter had stacks of homemade lemon butter and raspberry jam, and Mrs Gibson was selling trayloads of shortbread. I looked everywhere for some longbread but no one seemed to have made any.

The main street was blocked off at each end so that everybody had to leave their cars somewhere else, which gave the banners a chance to drop their dust back on anyone who walked beneath them.

We heard a loud whistle blowing from around the corner, past the hotel, and then a terrible groaning and wailing coming from the same place, and then out marched the Ballargo Highland Pipe Band, which would've been much better if the pipes had've been in the highlands instead of marching down our main street and frightening Mrs Armstrong's cat, again.

Everybody clapped and cheered, a bit like they did after *Mr Fixit Motors*, but not quite as loudly. All the boys from the town and everywhere else marched and strutted with the band, in front of it, behind it, and, in Bill's case, in the middle of it.   Until the man with the big bass drum hit him across the ear with one of his big bass drum sticks.

The band had a human bagpipe for a few minutes after that. If you can call little brothers human.

Behind the band came Sergeant Connally, riding his bicycle carefully through the dust and looking out for troublemakers, but Scratcher was up the front, out of sight, and no one would call Jingo a troublemaker. Bill was still too little to have come to the sergeant's notice yet, and most people thought he was adorable, anyway. So did I – I always wanted to hit him with a door.

The Niamong Fire Brigade's truck coughed along after the policeman, the firemen in their overalls and things standing on the running boards and waving to the crowd with their sacks, while a stream of water poured out of a hole in the tank that was supposed to be for putting out fires with. I bet that whenever they were called out to fight a fire they made sure that it was near a creek before they went, or that it was close to the fire station. Or that it was burning on someone's property that they didn't like all that much.

Trying not to walk in the wet bits the ladies of the CWA carried their banner behind the fire brigade, all looking very smug with themselves and smiling so much you could see their gums, which is only smug spelt backwards, because they'd just won the Mallee's best wholemeal scones contest. Whenever I hear that word (wholemeal) I think of Mrs Phelpps for some reason, but I can't quite work out why. Mum was in the CWA and she was walking with the others and doing a fair amount of talking, even to Mrs Phelpps, which wasn't something I'd want to do on a nice sunny day.

Dad was strolling along behind the CWA with most of the nurses from the Base Hospital, and he appeared to be enjoying himself quite a lot. I noticed that Mum kept looking at him, a bit of a frown trying to take over from her smile but not having all that much luck.

After them came the Ballargo Highland Pipe Band, again, which meant that the parade had finished, but then came Sergeant Connally and the fire brigade and the CWA and Dad and the nurses, and then they all came around again! Luckily the water had run out by then, but just about everyone had mud on their shoes or boots.

The last time around the band stopped at the end of the street, just outside the Lalor's Arms, and the rest of the marchers went off to wherever they were going, which was mainly to buy things from the stalls or to talk to people.

The band played lots of stuff which they probably thought was music and then, when the sun was right on top of us reminding us that it was the middle of summer, they stopped playing and went in to have lunch with Mr Bell.

We all wandered around, licking toffee apples and crunching honeycomb, and played a bit of chasey here and there when we felt like it.

'Ladies and gentlemen!'

It was Mr Cross, the richest man in Niamong. He owned the General Store and the grain store, where you bought feed for your chooks and other animals, and he even did funerals. He wasn't terribly keen on children and probably should've been a teacher, along with Mr Braden and Mrs Phelpps.

He was also the Shire President, whatever that meant. He was dressed up in a long black gown with a chain around his neck which reminded me about our bath plug, which is another one of those backwards and forwards words. I thought he was stupid wearing all those hot things, but groan-ups are like that sometimes.

"Sometimes" is not really right, either – they're like that most of the time.

'Ladies and gentlemen!!!' he shouted into the microphone. The loudspeaker wasn't loud enough but people started to notice the red face up on the platform and gradually the street grew more or less quiet.

'Ladies and gentlemen,' he said, running out of exclamation marks just as everybody began to listen.

'Ladies and gentlemen,' he said, sweat dripping off his face onto the microphone, making plops echo all over the street.

And then he talked to us for half an hour about how wonderful it was that we should be having our first Dust Festival and how wonderful it was that we lived in such a wonderful country, and how wonderful it was that we'd won the war, and how wonderful it was that the CWA had won the wholemeal scones competition (which was probably even harder than winning the war), and how wonderful it was that the Ballargo Highland Pipe Band had found time to come all the way over to Niamong (they were probably sent by everybody in Ballargo), and how wonderful it was that we had such a fine body of men as the intrepid Niamong Fire Brigade, and how wonderful it was to have the nurses and Dr Pendle up at the Base Hospital, and how wonderful it was to have such a brave policeman as Sergeant Connally who always did his duty, and I thought how wonderful it'd be if he stopped talking, which he did when the platform collapsed under him. Mr Manderson grabbed the microphone and declared the Festival open in the mess and we all cheered, even though we thought it'd opened in the morning when they had the parade.

The whole of the Dust Festival was being held in the main street. They'd decided not to use the Showgrounds, so that we wouldn't think it was to be like the Show, I suppose, or else they might've thought that we'd all get bored going to the Showgrounds twice a year and not go to either the Show or the second annual festival. As long as they had fairy floss at both they could've had both of them every week as far as we were concerned, but groan-ups don't understand about those kinds of things. They always think that we'd want to do or see whatever they wanted to see or do, which is why they arranged for what was going to happen after the parade to happen.

I noticed quite a few men walking around during the morning, wearing old army boots and shorts, and shirts with the sleeves ripped out. They seemed to be pretty strong – their muscles were even more taut than us school kids after year of Mr Braden – and they seemed to have a bit of trouble smelling the different kinds of jams and things being sold at the stalls beside the road. Another thing I noticed after a while was that hardly anyone seemed to go too close to any of them, and when I accidentally bumped into one of them after lunch I nearly fainted – it was like bumping into the McPhees, only different. I even discovered later that all the men actually *were* McPhees, or were married to a McPhee girl of one kind or another.

The best thing about them was that all of the rest of us stopped being bothered by the flies.

Everybody'd finished their hot sausages and pies (except for you-know-who), the mud was hardening up along the road where the water had been spilt on it, and the dust was making lots of little whirlwinds all over the place. Mr Brister and Scratcher's dad had managed to sort of fix up the platform, and the microphone was back on its stand, a little bent and muddy, waiting to be tapped, blown in to, and yelled at.

Which it was, right then.

'Ladies and gentlemen! Boys and girls!'

You can tell straight away that it wasn't Mr Cross this time, can't you. It was Mr Manderson, but you knew that anyway.

'Today we have something that's never been done anywhere else in the world before!'

I thought that might've been a bit of a tricky thing to say, but as I didn't have time to do any checking up right then I let him go on.

'As it's our first Dust Festival we thought we'd better organise something special, or no one'd pay any attention to us, and no-one would come.'

Why would anyone come, anyway, when no one knew what the something special was? I told you that groan-ups are a bit strange.

'Would you all please move to the sides of the road!'

All up and down the street people started to move over to the sides, jostling each other so that they didn't miss out on a good spot whilst trying not to knock over the stalls of food and things under the trees.

The only people who weren't going to the sides were the men I told you about before: they were heading up to where the road was roped off from the traffic. There

were about ten of them. No, there were eleven, twelve...
thirteen – Mr McPhee had joined them, and he was
wearing shorts and boots and a sleeveless shirt, too.

We watched them, wondering what they were doing
and hoping that the wind didn't spring up before they'd
finished. People seemed to be holding their breaths, as
though they were waiting for something to happen, and
they let them out when the men disappeared into the
crowd that suddenly parted in front of them.

'Ladies and gentlemen!! Girls and boys!!'

Mr Manderson was phoning the micro again.

'You've seen them! They've come from all over
Victoria! From Ballargo and Ballan! From Kyneton and
Colbinabbin! From Manangatang, and even from
Melbourne!'

That was most of the important places in the state. If
they'd all heard about us Niamong was certainly on the
map.

'Here they are, ladies and gentlemen! Racing against
each other for the first time, for the first time anywhere in
the world, the World's First Nightmans' Race!!!'

NIGHTmans' race?!?! I was so embarrassed! How
could I get away! The people who took away the...you

know, the…stuff…from our outside toilets. In cans. On their shoulders. Slopping…stuff…But I was jammed in the front row, with no escape, unless I went straight across the road and made everybody look at me!

The crowd up near the rope parted even more quickly than it had before. The men were coming back, in twos. Between them they were carrying a kind of a can, huge, glossy black, with handles. The cans were full to their brims. They put the six cans down on the road, in a line, and disappeared again somewhere. Nobody could believe it. Everybody was shouting at each other, and laughing, and saying things that were not really all that nice. Scratcher and Jemmy and Jingo and Noodles and the others were capering about in the middle of the street singing things that definitely weren't nice. My face burned.

The people parted again – it was like Moses and the Red Sea, only this time the sea was a different colour, and it wasn't the enemies who should've been drowned.

Another six cans joined the six already in line, and then out staggered Mr McPhee, carrying one by himself and slopping his boots, and upsetting a few flies on the way.

As soon as I'd realised that there were thirteen men I should've gone home. The festival was turning into a festerval.

'And now, ladies and gentlemen, the rules of the race! Our intrepid nightmen will form pairs. One person in each pair will carry the can to the other end and put it down there. He will then run back and get the other can, and take that one to the other end, too. His mate can help him, but he's not allowed to carry the can. When both cans are at the other end the men have to run back to this end. The first pair back is the winner!'

What about number thirteen? He'd forgotten Mr McPhee, who didn't have a pair, and I couldn't see anyone volunteering to help him.

'Oh, yes! We have a thirteenth contestant! Mr McPhee has bet all the others that he can beat them all hands down, on his own, without any help!'

Mr McPhee was probably pretty used to being on his own, except when he was at home, so that wasn't a real disadvantage.

'And nobody is allowed to wear a clothespeg on their nose!'

Smellbourne had come to Niamong.

'Are we ready, gentlemen?! Prepare to lift! Lift! Steady there, wait for it!'

We were all waiting for it, and hoping we wouldn't get it.

'GO!!'

The nightmen took off like a mob of nightmares, black cans on their heads bobbing in the sun like ancient battle chargers galloping into the fray. There wasn't all that much room for them and there were thirteen trying to get down to the end first. Stuff – you know, the stuff that, well, the stuff that goes in the toilet, was slopping all over the carriers and on to the helpers, and onto the road. There was pushing and shoving as they each tried to get in front, and more stuff slopped out of the cans. Their arms started to change colour and stuff dripped off their elbows, except for Mr McPhee – he was holding his can with both hands so the stuff slurped down his arms and into his shorts. They arrived at the other end in a jam and crashed the cans onto the road, sending plumes of stuff into their boots and onto a couple of kids who'd got a bit too close, to see what was in the cans. They ran off, screaming and holding their noses.

Back they raced, Mr McPhee trailling a little, squelching spray out of his boots. Up went the second cans, the men slipping a bit in the mud and wiping stuff off their faces. Off they all went, bunched up in a cloud of blowflies, pushing and shoving and jostling, running as fast as they could. Everybody was cheering them on and leaning backwards at the same time, and then the thirteen men and seven cans were flying and falling all over the place. People and stuff were going everywhere as the men lost their footing on a slippery part of the road.

But, hang on! What was that? I just saw a black cord or something stretching across the road from the platform to the other side, and on each end was a boy, and one boy's name was Scratcher and the other boy's name was...Jingo!

Cans were rolling everywhere, spilling everything all over the road, turning our main street into a creek of mud and horrible other stuff. Several men had their feet in cans and I couldn't see Mr McPhee at all because his can had changed its direction completely and was now upside down and covering his head and shoulders. He was running around like some strange sort of emu that'd had its head cut off, with stuff streaming down him and overflowing out of his boots. After a couple of seconds of this he started to lose his footing in the mud and then he somersaulted over someone and ended up with his feet in the air and his head in the can, still.

The platform collapsed for the second time that day and Mr Cross, who had foolishly climbed back on it to show how important he was, quickly made up Mr McPhee's pair. The black cord, which I think belonged to the loud speakers, had dropped back onto the road, and Jingo and Scratcher had disappeared, which was probably just as well for them.

Every time one of the men or Mr McPhee or Mr Cross stood up they fell down again. They were getting muddier and muddier and dustier and dustier and lots of other things as well and the rest of Niamong was laughing its head off and rolling around but not in the middle of the street.

No one would forget our first Dust Festival, which was also our last Dust Festival. We still had dust all the time, except when it was raining, but the groan-ups decided that the Show once a year was enough for our town to manage.

The crutches? Well, there were twenty-eight — two each for each of the men who joined in the great Nightmans' Race of Niamong.

And *you* can work out who they all were.

12

Bits and Pieces

...where I tell you about some interesting things.

I f you don't count sitting next to Jingo, the best place I know is Hanging Rock. It's a magic place, a craggy, mossy, full-of-secrets place, a place where this world disappears and you can disappear into a different world.

Around the bottom are great trees, the homes of koalas and rosellas. Spiny anteaters snuffle through the bracken and soft soil with their pink noses, hoping they won't find any spiny ants.

You can climb the rock from just about anywhere. The easy way is up the path, and that's the way to go with your Mum. It rises slowly through the trees so that she doesn't lose her breath too soon; steps are cut into the steeper bits, and she can stop at the tops of these and look down at the view, pretending that she isn't puffed out. Then it crams between huge boulders, with water oozing down the ones that are in the shade, and you can see tiny flowers in the moss.

Half way up is a sort of slopey flat spot where you can sit on a rock and get out your drink bottle before tackling the harder last stage to the top. This part isn't as far as the first part but it always takes longer, even without your mum or your little brother. It's mainly over or around rocks and boulders, and sometimes between them, or jumping across chasms from one boulder to another about a mile away.

I like going up the easy way sometimes, but I usually go up one of the hard ways, where there really isn't a path and you have to watch out that you don't step on any loose stones or slimy, slippery rocks. These ways are up the outside of Hanging Rock, instead of up into the middle, and you keep on coming to cliffs with narrow ledges that you have to inch along, your face rubbing against the rough stone and your heart trying to bump you off into the trees far below. You don't tell your mum about this.

When you get to the top of the old volcano you can see everywhere – the Camel's Hump in the way between Hanging Rock and Melbourne; the forest creeping up the ranges; valleys and hills; and green farms (in winter), and trees and tiny cattle; and the race course; and the road going all around the bottom.

Our tent was in the forest, where the trees broke against the Rock, tucked away from the wind. When we straggled back to camp after a day exploring the Rock the sun was falling into the far hills and wisps of mist were twining down the slope. Mum lit the fire for us to warm our hands and bodies, and Dad put on a billy of stew that I'd made the day before. The firelight flickered on the tree trunks, making everything go black behind them, and it turned the mist red and orange and yellow so that it looked like smoke coming from a rainbow.

I sat on a stool with my back against a rough-barked tree, looking into the fire, glad that I wasn't still up on the top of the Rock with the mist swirling around the dark boulders, when I thought I saw something white move between the trees. My skin suddenly crawled all over itself as I looked up quickly. But there was only darkness, and mist catching the light of the fire.

The others were quietly doing nothing when my skin suddenly twanged from my ear tips to my toes. There it was again! I could see it clearly this time. It was all white, and it was walking, or gliding, through the trees. I couldn't really see what it was before it disappeared down the hill, but then another white shape came, much closer this time, and I could see that it looked like a person, a girl, and she seemed to be wearing old-fashioned clothes – a long white dress and a wide-brimmed hat and she had an umbrella over her shoulder. I stared and stared and stared until she, too, disappeared, with a sad smile, after the first one.

I unfroze my eyelids and blinked and blinked. I didn't think the others had seen anything. Dad was stirring the stew. Mum was spreading butter on thick slices of bread. Bill was getting the plates out.

I ate the meal without saying anything, and the others hardly spoke, either. After we'd finished, Dad lit the pressure lantern in the tent and we climbed into our sleeping bags for the night.

And I read the last few pages of my book. *Picnic at Hanging Rock.*

*****

Watching Dad and the Reverend Mr Greensleeve playing chess is like watching two elephants in an arm-wrestling contest – you know something is happening, but you can't quite put your finger on what.

They spend about half an hour setting up the board, putting all the men in place – even the queen, though how you can call a queen a man is something that only grownups can understand, or, at least, they don't seem to worry about it.

First they decide who'll be black and who'll be white. This must be very important because one of them puts a black pawn in one hand and a white pawn in the other, and then the other person has to guess which hand has the white one. I always know which one it is, but Dad never gets it right and he nearly always chokes trying to stop Mr Greensleeve seeing how upset he is. After that momentous decision is all over they put the important pieces on the board first, on the squares nearest the players: the castles, the knights, the queen, the king, and the bishops. Mr Greensleeve usually puts the bishops on very carefully, and looks at the door to see if anyone's coming in. At about this time each time they play they have an argument about whether the king goes on a square that's the same colour as he is, or not. This also seems to be very important, but I can't see why. The pawns would be put on last, and they hardly worried about them at all, but when it came to starting the game there was always another argument about whether each pawn would be allowed to move one or two squares the first time, or only the first pawn could move one or two squares the first time, or whether all pawns were only allowed to move one square whenever they moved. You might be only a pawn, but that certainly never means that you never get into trouble!

The strangest thing about chess, though, is the respect that Dad and Mr Greensleeve gave to the king. As far as I could see the king was just about the most useless piece on the board – everybody else was there to protect him. Even the pawns were front line soldiers, going into battle against the enemy, capturing a prisoner if they were lucky, and sacrificing themselves for their side if they weren't. The castles could zip up and down the board and sideways and capture men when they weren't looking; knights on their steeds could jump over everyone and sneak up on an enemy without him knowing; and the bishops could spirit themselves diagonally backwards and forwards whenever they had a clear path.

All the king could do was move one space at a time, or cringe behind his brave and clever men. And the bravest and cleverest man wasn't a man anyway! The queen was the best of any of them: she could go forwards, as many squares as she liked; she could go backwards; she could go sideways; she could even go diagonally. The only thing she couldn't do was jump, but all the queens I know are far too ladylike to go jumping. Especially over men.

By the time they'd got the board all set up and stopped arguing about various things it'd be time for afternoon tea, so they'd stop for half an hour and eat their scones and cream and drink their tea, and Mr Greensleeve would tell Dad about all the things he'd left out of his sermons because he thought that the people wouldn't appreciate them, and Dad told him about all the things he'd left inside people during operations because he'd for-gotten to pull them out before he'd sewn up the wounds.

After that they'd finally get down to the game, staring for hours at the board before moving a piece, groaning when they had one of their men taken, and generally having a miserable time.

And when Dad finally got beaten, which was usually, he always looked around as though he should've been hanging from a cross, which was more in the Reverend Greensleeve's line, really.

*****

It was absolutely disgusting. Even though Bill was only two, Dad should never have done it: they were having a bath together! And they both had their clothes off! Why couldn't they behave properly? I suppose it was be-cause we were going through another drought and there wasn't enough water for everybody to have a bath on their own, but *I* certainly wasn't going to have a bath with Bill. Not after he did something in it once, which gave him a terrible fright.

Once when he was about four he asked me why he had to have a water-proof sheet under his ordinary sheet, and I'd told him that it was because he still wet his bed. He said, 'I can't help it. It just falls out.' And it did, nearly every night. Another time, when he was even younger, he was in Dad's surgery, when I heard this bit, which shows you how bad things got with both of them pretty early.

'Dad, my eyes are still watering.'

'Well, turn them off.'

'Dad, you're making silly sense. You're not sick, I am.'

I was really the sick one, sick of little brothers and sick of terrible jokes. Little brothers didn't know anything, either. Mum was trying to tell Bill that babies are born at the hospital, and that when they're born they come out of mummy's tummy. Bill said, 'Yes, and when I was a little egg you ate me!'

Everybody knows where babies come from, but it's a little hard to explain sometimes. I suppose that he wasn't all that bad, though, when he was little. Not all the time, anyway. Sometimes he was quite funny, even. The first time he recited a nursery rhyme I nearly fell out of the chair: 'Mary had a little lamb, its crease was flight as snow.'

He loved drawing pictures, especially of himself. One day he started to do one of these, first making a roundish thing that was the head, and then he drew a straight line down the page. 'That's my long leg,' he said. 'Have I got a long leg like that?' He pulled up his pants leg and looked. 'Yes, I've got a long leg like that.'

The worst time of all, though, when he was little, was when he was sitting in the lounge, listening to Kindergarten of the Air on the radio. He had with him our old training potty. A few days before he'd said that he was going to wash one of my dolls in it, but I didn't believe him. I walked into the lounge room and couldn't believe my eyes. I rushed into the kitchen and yelled at Mum and Dad, 'Bills doing wees in the pot and filling it over!!' Dad went into the lounge to see for himself. After all, how could Bill fill the pot without it going all over the floor? Bill was just sitting there. 'No, he's not, Liss,' said Dad, and he went back into the kitchen. As soon as he'd gone, Bill stood up and I could see that he had! And then he started to wash one of my best dolls in it!! I screamed and yelled and Mum and Dad rushed back in, but all they did was laugh!

And Mum said something about saving water in the drought.

I was out walking along the railway line one day, not long after breakfast, when I looked up and saw the most wonderful thing I'd ever seen in the sky.

There were many long, dark clouds up there, made even darker by the early morning sun coming up behind them, and a hole grew between the different black clouds.

Through the hole I could see a white cloud, much higher in the sky. The sun caught this one and gradually turned it pink. And then green edges circled the pink. Slowly it turned into a cloud rainbow – at one end it was a kind of sandy yellow, then came pink and reddish, and then blues and greens and purples. And then the cloud got whiter and whiter, and the colours faded in the brilliant sunlight and disappeared as the sun torched directly through the hole, and I had to look away. Things like that happen to me all the time. It's the same with words. I like doing things with words, inventing new ones, or turning them inside out. Here's a new one for you: craxy. It means not quite crazy – can you see why? And what about dam? That's only mad spelt backwards, which is what you get if you fall into one with your clothes on. And I've even discovered the only word in the world that you can turn into its opposite by moving only one letter. The word is united, and you can work out what its opposite is.

The best thing I've ever done, though, is to turn words into a sword, or a sword into words, and you can't get much cleverer than that, can you? Dad likes playing with words, too, but the only trouble with him is that he tries to make them into jokes, and nobody can understand them. One day he came out of his surgery, almost bursting, and yelled at Mum: 'What do they call a sore throat in Russia?!' Mum didn't seem all that interested in Russian sore throats.

'Leningitis!!' yelled Dad, and Russia-ed back into the surgery, just ahead of a carrot.

After we'd been learning about France in school one day he put on his know-all look and asked me what French policemen were called. Well, everyone knew that they were called gendarmes, so I told him. He looked pleased that I'd got that one right, then he started to frown.

'Very good, Liss. But what do you call a stupid French policeman?'

I wracked my brains. I couldn't remember Mr Braden saying anything about stupid French policemen, or stupid anything else, for that matter. Apart from a few with Scratcher.

'I don't know, Dad. What is a stupid French policeman called?' It's always best to give in quickly, or you could be there all night, hoping for a dying patient to ring up.

'It's easy! He's called a......gen*dumb*!!'

What can you do about fathers??

*****

'Will you Please GeT out of the Way.'

It was one of those Capital Letter People again. I still hadn't worked out how they did it with their voices, but I was getting Pretty Good at it when I was writing my Stories.

'I said to GeT out of the Way!'

Actually she'd capital Pd Pleased as well when she said that, but that sounds a bit rude, so I won't say it

'Get Out of My Way at Wunce!'

The deep voice seemed to be getting a bit angry, and was forgetting how to spell. Not that spelling mattered all that much when you were saying something, or being angered at.

You just said whatever sounded most sensible at the time, and hoped that you'd got the meaning right in time to make sure that nothing happened to your bottom.

'For the LasT Time, I SaiD GeT Out of My Way!'

Did you hear thaT? Capital letters at the Start of words *and* at the enD! I had to see who this person was, and what was causing all the fuss.

I rushed around the corner full pelt, which was a dumb thing to do because I crashed straight into a flowered mountain that was even bigger than Mrs Phelpps on one of her bad days. It was Mrs Cross, Mr Cross's Mrs Cross, the Mr Cross who had the Can on his HeaD, the Mr Cross who was the Richest Man in Niamong. Which meant that she was the Richest Woman in Niamong and I suddenly remembered Dad's awful joke about woe to man and wondered if it meant woe to young girls as well, because I was flat on my back on the footpath, which is not the best place in the world to be when a mountain decides to fall on you.

'What do You MeaN By CraSHing InTo Me Like ThaT!'

Now it was capitals in the MIDDLE of words! It was worth lying on the ground to hear that! I had so much to learn if I was going to be a proper grown-up one day.

'I'm sorry, Mrs Cross! I just wanted to see who was...I mean I wanted to see what...'

'StoP Mumbling, chilD! And GeT uP from thaT StUpiDPosition!'

The capitals were jumping out of her mouth like spitfires, little black furies that started to drench me.

'Mrs Cross! I thought that I could Help.'

I'd done it! I'd put a capital at the beginning of a word! Anybody could put capitals at the beginnings of people's names, but I'd put one at the start of "help!"

'There was So much Noise that I thought I'd better See if I could do Something!'

It was getting easy!

'I NeeD HelP, I'll CalL for IT! I Don't NeeD a Young Pipsquich!'

I wasn't sure whether I'd spelt that last word right anyway because I was too busy thinking about my next capitals.

'I Didn't Mean any HarM, Mrs Cross.'

I'd got one at the end of a word!

'That Doesn't Matter. You StiLL BumPed inTo Me!'

'I know. I was JusT Walking Down the StreeT when I hearD a LoT of Noise and I THoughT thaT someone was inTrouble.'

'It's Very Wrong and Silly to Run around Corners like thaT, though'

'Yes, I kNow. I Don't think THat I'LL Do iT aGain, Mrs CRoss.'

'Well, I'm very Pleased to hear That.'

'I Was Very SoRRy to See Mr Cross Get ThaT Can Emptied on his Head aT the DuST FesTival...'

'Oh, dear, so was I. He StanK for a WEEK! Can You ImaGine THAT! Yes, and I maDe him sleeP in the spare room ouT the back, I Can tell You!'

'I Don't BLAme You, Mrs Cross. I Would Have DoNe EXactly the SaMe!'

'You seem to be a very Nice Girl, Liss. Come in for a cup of T.'

*****

Why *is* life different for girls?

Why aren't we treated exactly the same as boys? After all, we see things exactly the same way, through our eyes, and we smell things exactly the same way, through our noses, and we feel things exactly the same way, through our skins. And we hear things the same way, and we have two legs the same as boys, and two arms, and two . . . no, there's a bit of a difference. Yes, and there are one or two other differences as well, which you'll have to think of yourself, because I'm certainly not going to write about them here.

And why don t boys have to wear skirts? You never see boys wearing skirts, except for Scotsmen, and they don't really count. Skirts are much more comfortable than shorts, because they don't get too tight around your legs, and they let the cool air in in summer. And boys ought to have to have long hair, because long hair looks really nice, especially with a bright ribbon or two, or plaits. And when they grow up they should be made to wear make-up, and high heels, and lovely long evening dresses swishing across dance floors.

I suppose life is different for girls because we *are* different.

We're better.

But don't tell Jingo.

Did you enjoy reading *Lissie Pendle*?

I'd love you to write a review, at

http://www.lulu.com/spotlight/ianburns

Books by Ian Burns

All works are available as eBooks.

Ranga Plays Australia

It's only four years after the end of World War 2, during which there were no great cricket matches. But now things are getting back to normal: the Australians have thrashed the Poms in England (which is always, and will always be, a good thing), India has played its first Test series in Australia, and 'the Don' has retired.

In a small Bangalore village young Ranganathan Rao is musing about life in general and cricket in particular. The weather's been hot and dry for ever – everyone's eyes are skywards, looking for the monsoon. Except for Ranga's, whose spinning fingers begin to itch.

Kumar, Ranga's English/Geography/History teacher, as part of a discourse on the strangeness of the English language, introduces his pupils to an especially strange word - that he heard an Australian say during the war – and invites them to try to pronounce it and identify its meaning. After many unsuccessful attempts Kumar reveals both the word's pronunciation and meaning, and suggests that everyone might remember this, as one day they might go to Australia.

This starts Ranga thinking.

Thomas Bulford's English Companion

An extraordinary book, giving seminal insights into such diverse matters as Amazons and aardvarks, and the mythical or legendary Eve (of Eden), Helen (of Troy), and Joan (of Arc).

Of great importance is the book's twenty-seven categories, each with a short essay purportedly by the author, introducing each section.

Saying anything else, at this stage, would be entirely superfluous, and probably an insult.

Thomas Bulford's Essays on Life, Language & Love

Readers may be aware that Thomas Bulford died recently (though not as recently as before), and that I had what I then regarded as the onerous honour of editing his lexicographical work.

Following this, his son – Thomas Bulford Junior II – presented the Publisher (whom even I now acknowledge the need to capitalise) with a box of scribblings that he said were his 'distinguished' father's.

On being shown these, my impression was that they were, indeed Thomas Bulford's (the senior, that is), for two reasons, though not without reservation (as some of them do appear to be at least a little out of character with the bulk of the *opus*).

Firstly, they bore a striking resemblance to the 'essays' that the Publisher insisted on being incorporated in the *English Companion* as introductions to the various definitional categories.

Secondly, and I say this with as much grace as I can, they, whilst being somewhat idiosyncratic in construction and questionable in logic, contained a number of insights into the human condition that were also occasionally present in the earlier volume.

Accordingly, with less reluctance than before, I agreed to edit this material, and offer it to readers for their judgement. *Editor*

The Alone Man

The Alone Man draws on the concept of 'dreamtime', the Australian aboriginal mythology of creation and relationships to and custodianship of the land. It is a 'double love story' about a man's love for his wife and family and his love of the land and nature.

Set in outback Australia around 100 years ago, the story is of a simple man in a simpler time creating a micro-world as many pioneers did. He carves a farm out of the bush, courts and weds a girl from even farther out back, and raises a family.

Although he doesn't realise it, his life is a kind of poetry, with the beauty of love, of nature, and of sorrow as the themes. The book affirms all of these, and the continuity of life.

A 'prose poem' which is poetic about something as ordinary (or common) as building a life – marriage, birth, death, livelihood. The style is gentle and poetic, and the story is, at the same time, humorous and sad, touching and poignant, affirming and happy, dreamy and warm.

The Alone Man is a simple story full of understated insights that will have deep emotional resonance with readers – male and female, old and young – all over the world.

The Wisdom of Harkishen Singh

Little is known about Sardarji Harkishen Singh, other than that he left the Punjab at the time of what he called *The Troubles*. He eventually found himself in Akkithimmanalli, where he befriended young Ranganathan Rao.

The sayings recorded in these pages would undoubtedly have been lost if it hadn't been for a series of accidents – all cricket related – whereby the guru's child companion became a close friend of the compiler of this volume.

To this day, long after his village turned into the great city of Bengaluru and his guru pyred into the infinite tomorrow, Ranga *still* has not confidently resolved the meanings of all these pieces of fondly-remembered wisdom.

But, as he said in his biography: *Wisdom, to be wise, is not always of the understandable kind.*

A compilation of sayings – sometimes wise, sometimes inscrutable, sometimes humorous – of an Indian guru in post-WW2 India, as spoken to and recalled by his young protégé.

FOR CHILDREN

Lissie Pendle

Lissie Pendle is about trouble. But not trouble with a capital T. It's trouble which just...well, it just happens. Usually with the help of her little brother, or Scratcher and his friends, or just....things. Lissie is busy, pre-occupied, if you like, coping with events and trying to sort out and put in their proper place (ie beside and slightly in awe of her) the various eligible boys of the town. In these endeavours she succeeds quite gloriously, although she's actually the only person who understands this.

In the course of telling us about a number of pretty unusual events, such as the case of the killer koala, or what happened in old-fashioned trains' toilets, or when she met a lady who inserted capital letters into her conversation, or when there was blood instead of ink in the inkwell, or....well, a pile of other things, we discover an Australia of another time.

When things were clear, including the air, and life was simpler and, yes, funnier.

Possum and Python

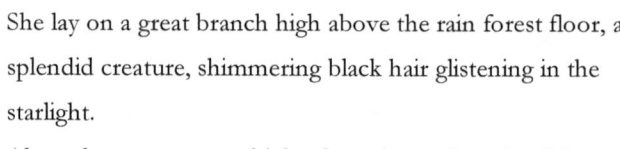

She lay on a great branch high above the rain forest floor, a splendid creature, shimmering black hair glistening in the starlight.

Above her, on an even higher branch, *another* splendid creature, a mortal enemy.

She didn't know it was there, and it wasn't interested in her, but an extraordinary adventure was about to begin – a tale of surprise, dedication, and, above all, love (which, as we all know, can change the world).

Ranga Plays Australia

It's only four years after the end of World War 2, during which there were no great cricket matches. But now things are getting back to normal: the Australians have thrashed the Poms in England (which is always, and will always be, a good thing), India has played its first Test series in Australia, and 'the Don' has retired.

In a small Bangalore village young Ranganathan Rao is musing about life in general and cricket in particular. The weather's been hot and dry for ever – everyone's eyes are skywards, looking for the monsoon. Except for Ranga's, whose spinning fingers begin to itch.

Kumar, Ranga's English/Geography/History teacher, as part of a discourse on the strangeness of the English language, introduces his pupils to an especially strange word - that he heard an Australian say during the war – and invites them to try to pronounce it and identify its meaning. After many unsuccessful attempts Kumar reveals both the word's pronunciation and meaning, and suggests that everyone might remember this, as one day they might go to Australia.

This starts Ranga thinking.

Scratcher

Have you ever wondered why clocks have hours, and minutes, and seconds…but not firsts?

You will not find the answer to this question in this book, but Scratcher will tell you what happens if

your dog goes wild in a butcher's shop,

or if an eel gets up your trouser leg when you're standing in the middle of the creek in the rain,

or if you fall in love with your teacher.

And he'll tell you about the McPhees, and his friends, and about the cat whose feet never touch the floor,

and what happened when a swan's EGG learnt to fly, and about the world's only fat butter of a dog,

and…and…and, well about one or two other things as well…

Nearly 5,000 copies sold.

The Day and Night Machine

It's Jess's thirteenth birthday. She's been in bed for nearly a year, the result of a car accident that killed her father.

Surprisingly, she finds a birthday present from her father, an unusual gift for a girl and one which she, her grandfather, and her mother, puzzle over.

In the course of playing with it she discovers that it has some highly-unexpected properties.

But then, purely by accident, she discovers its most amazing feature.

She wonders how she can use this for the benefit of the world, but is foiled by Miss Sturzen, a villainous redhead, who steals the 'machine' for her own enrichment and evil ends.

When she captures and imprisons Jess, she has a clear run, but Jess is able to circumvent her difficulties and come up with a particularly appropriate counter strategy, aided by a phlegmatic police sergeant and his retinue of puppies.

Miss Sturzen is arrested and taken away, but escapes and returns to wreak mortal revenge on Jess, using a day and night machine. Unfortunately for her, however, things don't quite go to plan.

And then we discover the *real* reason for Jess's father's gift.

The Package on the Tram is Jess's next adventure.

The Package on the Tram

The world's largest dog that vanishes or re-appears out of nowhere, with hairs larger than trees.

Creatures larger than mammoths that can help the tiniest.

A cobweb that changes colour according to whether...

Where Jess can be killed at any moment by anyone she loves, and who love her.

And a decision that leads to a desperate loss.

A mystery story involving a thirteen-year old girl, her unwanted visitor, her mother and grandfather, three detectives, a man of two tribes, and a bunch of Labradors with colour-coded collars.

Oh, and a father who may not be really there...

The Search for Quong

Quong was a creature of the olden olden days, even before grandmother.

He was a short fellow, or, at least, that's what they said, with long, thin legs and an even longer, thinner tail. His face was fat and wrinkly, and big bushy eyebrows kept out the sun and flies.

At least that's what I think he looked like, though no–one has actually seen him that I'd believe. Which, of course, was the trouble.

Some people say that there are no such things as quongs, that it's a stupid name, and that if there were any there'd be pink elephants, too.

But those people don't think Father Christmas comes every year, either.

Of course this is all nonsense. There must be quongs and we must find them.

And, if this story's any good, we will.

Twevven and the big bigger biggest baby burp

Twevven has forgotten his purse so finds himself 'volunteering' to do something that he's never done before. It is fairly certain that he ends up regretting this.

Twevven in a very dangerous situation

It's a very hot day, so Twevven decides to go to the beach. When he gets there he sees that it's terribly crowded. He then makes a seriously foolish decision. If you ever take a child to the beach you need to read this story first, and discuss what Twevven did wrong and how everything turned out all right in the end.

To find out more about Ian's published works, including previews, please visit
http://www.twevven.com
Email: ibgburns@gmail.com